WIND IN THE SAGE
by
Christine Bennett

To the boys and girls from the big cities who came
to spend their vacations at the Lightning W Ranch
near the town of Tincup, Arizona, fifteen-year-old
Betty Stone, who lived there the year round, seemed
to have the most wonderful life imaginable. Bettty,
as a would-be artist, did appreciate the natural beauty
of the desert country, the big sky and the vast range.
But she felt her ambition could never be completely
fulfilled until she had studied art in a metropolis filled
with fine museums.

Therefore her Aunt Mary's invitation to spend a
year in Chicago was like the answer to a dream. And
Betty's parents' decision that the offer had to be refused, and that dreams had to be earned, made the
girl profoundly unhappy.

WIND IN THE SAGE

Wind in the Sage

By

CHRISTINE BENNETT

Alouette CONTEMPORARY TEENS *Romance*

By

Sharon Publications, Inc.
Closter, NJ

Copyright © MCMLXII by Arcadia House
Published by
Sharon Publications Inc.
Closter, N.J. 07624
Printed in the U.S.A.
Cover illustrations by Will Harmuth
ISBN 0-89531-144-5

WIND IN THE SAGE

Chapter 1

It seemed important to Betty Stone that all the evidence and every statement be investigated carefully before the Students' Disciplinary Board recommended a course of action to the principal. So although she disliked contention, Betty rose when it was her turn to speak and said as tactfully as she could: "Madam President, I think that a decision at this time would be premature. Frankly, I'm confused. One person says one thing, another person says he's a liar, and still another person says something else. But so far no one has convinced me that this or that person is guilty beyond all question of doubt. For that reason, I'd be definitely reluctant to recommend something so serious as suspension. There are only about ten more weeks in the school year. Those are vital weeks if you're trying to bring your grades up. If Mary Foley and Ben Jorgenson were suspended now, they'd probably flunk their final exams. Wouldn't that be a shame, particularly if they're really innocent?"

Naturally, some of the kids resented her remarks. Three hands shot up, and Eloise Quayle buttressed her bid for recognition with the plea: "Cora, honey, please let me answer her."

The wonderful thing about Cora McHattie, though, was that she tried to be fair to everyone. "Pipe down," Cora told Eloise. "First of all, you're out of order. Secondly, I must say that I think Betty's points are well taken. How can we make a fair decision if we don't conduct an investigation of our own? We've heard all sides of the argument. But what do we really know except that one person thinks this and another thinks that?"

"Just the same," Eloise said, "I have the right to be heard."

Cora nodded to Minna Stagg. "Your hand went up first, Minna, so the chair recognizes you."

Obviously pleased with her cleverness, Minna said promptly: "Madam President, I yield the floor to Eloise Quayle."

Everyone laughed, Cora loudest of all. Always a good sport, Cora pointed her gavel at Eloise and sat down.

Eloise stood up and looked at her notes for a moment. She then removed her reading glasses and proceeded to speak in a quiet but deadly way about the testimony the Board had sat receiving all that afternoon. To Betty, it was both interesting and instructive to hear Eloise develop her argument, for Eloise had an excellent command of English and a real talent for organization. Moreover, Eloise always expressed herself positively, so that if you were not on guard she tended to make you believe she was stating proven facts rather than giving you her personal opinion.

And how effectively Eloise stated her so-called facts; how damagingly she summarized them!

"Item one," Eloise said: "Mary Foley and Ben Jorgenson have given identical answers to all test questions during the past two months.

"Item two: Mary Foley and Ben Jorgenson have jumped from the average-student list to the honor-student list during the past two months.

"Item three: Mary Foley and Ben Jorgenson made their phenomenal leap to the honor-student list only after Ben was discovered in the principal's office one afternoon two months ago.

"Item four: Mary Foley and Ben Jorgenson have refused to take tests designed to clue the faculty in on their basic knowledge.

"And last but not least," Eloise concluded,

"there isn't a kid in Tincup Union High School who will tell you that Mary Foley and Ben Jorgenson study worth a darn. So if all this isn't conclusive evidence, I would like to know what is. What are we supposed to do: declare them innocent because none of us happened to be in the principal's office when Ben Jorgenson got copies of the exam questions for the whole term? I'm not at all confused, as some people seem to be. I think Mary Foley and Ben Jorgenson are guilty of having cheated and I think it's our duty to recommend their suspension. In fact, Madam President, I make a motion to that effect here and now."

Minna Stagg seconded the motion promptly, and someone called the question and cut off further debate before Betty could argue the matter. Cora, under obligation to call for a vote, did her duty. Of the nine members of the Students' Disciplinary Board, only Betty refused to support the recommendation for suspension. Cora, who had no legal right to vote except to break a deadlock in case of a tie, was clearly unhappy about the whole thing. "Poor guys," she said, "their folks will skin them alive. Too bad. Okay, the decision has been made and that's that. Eloise, will you write the letter to Mr. Henshaw? Watch your grammar, though. Guess who's student supervisor for the month?"

"Mrs. McCracken?"

"Yup."

Eloise's eloquent shudder made everyone laugh. Betty thought of telling her that in this case the punishment certainly suited Eloise's crime, but she never spoke the words for fear someone would call her a poor loser. After Cora had closed the meeting, Betty congratulated Eloise on her brilliant presentation of her argument. "I still think you're wrong," she said, choosing her words carefully, "but here and now I'll concede you're the top debater in the school."

Eloise frowned. "Hey, I'm not sure I like

the implication it was my tongue that convicted them. All I did was present the facts."

Betty left it at that. She got her books from under her chair and hustled outdoors. Because the meeting had lasted far longer than she had thought it would, she was agreeably surprised to find Jimmy Hayes still waiting for her. Grinning, she tossed him her books. "You must be in love," she joshed him. "Fancy waiting all this time when you could have been hitting home runs or something on the ball field."

"You want a clout?"

Betty marched straight up to him and thrust her chin out. "Go ahead and clout me," she challenged. "I defy you to clout me!"

"You're crazy," Jimmy said. "Living way off there in the desert on your folks' ranch has turned you loco."

"It *isn't* the desert. We may be near the desert, but we're not on it. Don't you know anything about the West? What idiots city boys can be!"

Jimmy led her to his car and opened the door for her. He mumbled something or other about not having had the car long enough to repair the upholstery and give the interior the cleaning it needed. Betty told him a white lie to wipe the embarrassment off his handsome face. "Cleanest car I've ever ridden in," she fibbed. "It was darned nice of you to wait, too. I wasn't looking forward to the long ride home on a rented horse."

He was astonished. "You mean you actually would have rented a horse and ridden off alone across that desert?"

"Well, why not?"

After he had gotten in under the steering wheel, Jimmy let his breath out. "Now I've heard everything," he said. "I guess your folks must be loco, too. Where do we go next?"

"To the jailhouse. I promised Mom to give old Mr. Swiftfoot the scolding of his life. It won't do a bit of good, but a promise is a promise. Know where the jailhouse is?"

"Believe it or not, I do."

"Then we go to the ranch," Betty announced. "The folks look you over and approve. You have a nice swim in our pool. You have some of the tastiest food you'll ever eat in Arizona. Finally, you get onto one of our horses and go riding with me to watch the moon come up over the range."

"Guess again," Jimmy said. "Here's one fellow you'll never get onto any horse."

Jimmy started the old Chevrolet sedan. Although the street was always all but deserted on Saturdays, he checked to make certain there was no oncoming traffic before he turned the car out onto the road. He drove at about twenty miles per hour to the junction of Tumbleweed Road and Jackrabbit Way. There he made a right-hand turn for the two-mile drive straight through the center of the old town to the adobe jailhouse near Sourwater Creek. Significantly,

he asked no questions about the outcome of
the Board meeting, reporter though he was.
Instead, he chattered amusingly about
horses and the fear he had had of them ever
since an afternoon in New York City when
a horse had knocked him down. "I was four
at the time," Jimmy explained. "I must have
yelled up quite a storm, because adults came
running from all directions. I hate to tell you
this, but you couldn't bribe me to mount
a horse. Now ask me why my folks came
west to Arizona."

"Well, why did they?"

"My father grew tired of being a big-city
surgeon. He said he wanted to be a small-
town doctor, a general practitioner. About
three months ago I wouldn't have given you
a plugged nickel for this town of Tincup. All
anybody ever talks of is ranch life."

"But you discovered we're not so bad
after all?"

Jimmy smiled. "Nope. I got this job with
Mr. Bourke of the *Tincup Ledger*. He's a

fine man to work for, to learn from. And I'm learning, I think. For instance, I no longer think it strange for you to associate with a dirty jailbird Indian. Mr. Bourke explained that he used to pack you around with him like a papoose. Mr. Bourke also explained that was a remarkable thing for an Indian man to do."

Betty pointed to her honey-gold hair. "This explains the mystery, Jimmy. Mr. Swiftfoot hadn't seen many children with blonde hair. He took a fancy to me, and he was so good to me Mom kept him around to look after me while she was busy with other chores. But he's had it now. Stealing horses! At his age! Why, he must be seventy years old!"

"Care to bet?" Jimmy asked. "From what I've heard from the kids, you're pretty loyal to your friends."

"Well, you have to be loyal, it seems to me. Just the same, there *are* limits."

But when they reached the one-story

adobe jail building on Sourwater Creek they found Mr. Swiftfoot looking so glum that Betty's vow to be tough with him melted like ice on a hot stove. While Jimmy sat in the office chatting with Constable Elliott, Betty led the old man out to the little walled exercise yard and gave him the corncob pipe and package of tobacco her father had sent "for old time's sake." Old Mr. Swiftfoot got the pipe into action in jig time. "Heap good," he said. "Father of Golden Hair heap friend."

Betty had to laugh. "And you're heap old faker," she said. "Mr. Swiftfoot, will you please stop using pidgin English? You speak better English than our English teacher, and you know it."

"Me in jail. Me hate white man. No speakum white man lingo in jail."

"Well, no wonder you're in jail! How many horses did you steal?"

Mr. Swiftfoot held up three fingers proudly.

Betty was scandalized. "There's nothing lower than a thief!" she scolded. "You've told me that yourself!"

"Want um ride, took um horses."

Betty sighed, wondering what on earth she was to do with him. Now that her mother had figuratively washed her hands of Mr. Swiftfoot, the old Indian was her responsibility. But how could a girl only fifteen and a half compel a man almost five times her age to behave properly? If she scolded him, she would certainly be told by someone that she ought to show more respect for her elders. But if she did not scold him, if she allowed him to do whatever he wanted, he would get into trouble over and over again. Worse, he would not eat intelligently or ever take baths or ever do a bit of useful work.

Betty nibbled thoughtfully at her lower lip, a juvenile habit she had not yet managed to break. Eventually her thinking produced what to her seemed a good idea. Deliberately, she forced as much anger as she could into her big, wide-spaced brown eyes. "Well," she told Mr. Swiftfoot, "I certainly can't help a thief. I couldn't respect myself if I did. After all, I have a code, too. I'm sorry, but that's how it is."

Mr. Swiftfoot grunted and sat down and crossed his legs Indian fashion. "Powwow," he ordered.

Betty shook her head vigorously. "No, sir. I hate to seem rude, but it seems to me you're not in any position right now to tell anyone what to do. We'll have to do things my way. First, you'll have to tell me where you put those horses. Then you'll have to write a letter to Mr. Lucas, telling him you're very sorry and promising to behave. Otherwise you'll have to stay here."

"Lucas bad man. No make treaty with Lucas."

Betty almost argued with him. But knowing from experience that he could be very deaf when he wished to be, she clamped her mouth shut and walked back across the exercise yard to the jail building.

The trick worked!

Speaking perfect English suddenly, Mr. Swiftfoot told her where the horses were and promised to write Mr. Lucas a letter of apology!

Chapter 2

Her success at the jailhouse left Betty better pleased with the results of the afternoon's activities. When she got back into the car her eyes were sparkling so happily that Jimmy asked if Mr. Swiftfoot had told her where to find buried gold. That reminded Betty of a story.

"We did find gold once," she told Jimmy. "I was ten at the time, and Mom was afraid I'd develop into a real tomboy. I went everywhere with Mr. Swiftfoot in those days. Right after school we'd saddle up and gallop over the range to Lonesome Butte. Well, one afternoon we decided to explore Rustlers' Creek. We must have followed it for three miles, climbing higher and higher into the hills. Suddenly something whizzed past my head, and then I heard the crack of a rifle. We hit the ground in a hurry, I'll tell you. And Mr. Swiftfoot was hopping mad. He made me follow him, and we wriggled like snakes until we reached a big rock. Mr. Swiftfoot made me wait there, and then he went on to find the person who had tried to shoot us. He never did find the man, but he did find the signs of the man's camp. While we were poking around, I found a prospector's pan down near the creek. There was gold in it, all right, but not very much. I guess everyone in Tincup has tried his luck at the creek, but all anyone ever gets is maybe four or five grains of gold to reward him for some darned hard work."

"Were you scared?" Jimmy asked. "I suppose not. I suppose you were too young to realize you could have been killed."

Betty said truthfully: "I really wasn't

afraid, but not for the reason you think. Dad started to train me to handle a gun when I was about six. I knew darned well what a gun could do because I'd seen some of the cowboys go after rattlesnakes. No, the reason I wasn't scared is that I knew it was just a warning shot. I wasn't the top marksman in the world, but even at that time I couldn't have missed the big target we made as we were riding along."

They reached the eastern end of town. Now for as far ass they could see only rangeland lay before them, seemingly endless miles of sage and ranch grass and browse, with here and there splotches of pin-cushion cactus and sunburned rocks and early spring flowers to delight the eye unexpectedly. Betty loved the view.

Jimmy surprised her by asking: "Want to go to the Lazy L Ranch first? I know where it is. The other day Mr. Bourke sent me out to talk to Mr. Lucas about that new ranchhouse he's building. Talk about elegant!

He's even going to have a rumpus room with a big mural on one of the walls. He's hired Mr. Lockwood to paint it, you know."

"I definitely know. I made a sketch for Mr. Lucas almost two months ago. Each of the kids in the art class did a sketch. Mr. Boykin thought that Mr. Lucas might select mine. But he chose Mr. Lockwood, just as most people thought he would."

"How old are you?" Jimmy asked.

"Closer to sixteen than fifteen."

Jimmy smiled sympathetically. "Say, I know just how it is! The first thing Mr. Bourke asked me was my age. When I told him I hit sixteen last November and had a license to drive, he said all right, he'd hire me. Then he apologized for having asked the question. He explained that he didn't want a scatty kid around the printing press-es. I guess Mr. Lucas was afraid to take a chance on a teen-age artist when he could hire an adult."

"Something like that, I suppose." But for

some reason Betty did not like the tone or wording of that remark. She added so Jimmy would not misunderstand: "And of course, maybe Mr. Lockwood knows much more about painting than I. Frankly, I don't like his paintings, but Mom tells me they're pretty good."

After they had traveled two miles across the range, the car went up a small grade to Shadow Mesa, and for the first time Jimmy Hayes began to look interested. "Sort of pretty," he conceded. "What's that red stuff growing over there?"

Betty looked and grinned. "Indian paint brush. You'll see lots of color around here in another few weeks. We've had an unusually wet spring. See that curl of smoke over near the hills? That's the Lightning W Ranch. My great-grandfather homesteaded there. The day he reached it there was a whopper of a thunderstorm, which explains the 'lightning' part of the name. The 'W' stands for the whoa my great-grandfather called to his team when he saw the grass and the water in the valley."

"When was that?"

"Shortly after the Civil War. My grandfather and father were born here."

"Been lived on a long time, hasn't it? Sort of gives you roots, if you know what I mean."

It seemed to Betty that Jimmy sounded wistful for roots of that kind. She asked no questions, however, but went right on talking about the ranch.

"Back in the old days," she explained, "everything was just cattle. Everybody seemed to want meat, and the range was really good then, not cluttered up with cedar as some of it is now. But by the time my grandfather took charge, things were changing here. We have about five hundred acres of alfalfa, for example, and others have even more. Most ranchers began to grow hay and other things because soon there was more cattle for sale than the country really needed. We grow cotton and cane now, too, and Dad is talking about trying some citrus fruit. What it all amounts to, Dad says, is that land is made to be worked, to be used. We certainly use ours. We run a dude ranch for kids in the summer, for instance."

They came to the first of the Lightning W drift fences, a simple affair constructed of posts and three strands of barbed wire. Betty got out and opened the gate, beginning to feel a bit excited and just a bit nervous because Jimmy was the first city boy she had ever brought home with her from school. She wondered what he would think of the ranch, and then she wondered what her folks and the cowboys and field hands would think of Jimmy. The cowboys in particular could be darned salty when they disliked someone. And heaven help poor Jimmy if they disliked him! The first time he went riding they would make sure he was mounted on a lively horse only an experienced person could ride!

Betty shivered. When the ranchhouse was in sight, she did something she had never done before to protect anyone. "You stick close to me," she warned, "this first time. No matter what a cowboy tells you, don't you dare get onto a horse until I give you the nod."

"Why not?"

"Because to them you're a dude, Jimmy, a dressed-up greenhorn from the big city of New York. The cowboys are wonderful men, but they do love to pull tricks on dudes."

Jimmy said crisply: "I can take care of myself. Maybe I'm not the greenhorn they may think I am."

Betty was dubious that he could take care of himself under all circumstances, but she did have to admit to herself about twenty minutes later that Jimmy knew how to meet strangers easily and help everyone overcome the awkwardness that always followed introductions. After her mother had shaken Jimmy's hand and welcomed him to the Lightning W Ranch, Jimmy marched straight across the big living room to look at the great oil painting over the fireplace mantel. "Say," Jimmy exclaimed, "that's darned good. Betty, did you paint that?"

Betty flushed and said that she had painted it but that she expected to do better some day. Jimmy at once said she might do as well but not better. The next thing Betty knew, she was standing under the picture and pointing out to Jimmy the many goofs she had made. She particularly called his attention to the way the Indian in the painting was brandishing his tomahawk. "There's my biggest goof," she said. "You try holding a tomahawk that way and you'll see what I mean. When Mr. Swiftfoot saw that picture the first time, he looked me straight in the eye and said: 'Baloney!' I could have screamed, I was so angry. But he was right, of course."

Her mother came in from the kitchen with tall glasses of Seven-Up for what she was pleased to call "the typically thirsty throats of magpies." Interestingly, her mother then sat down in the wing chair before the fireplace and asked Betty outright about the decision made by the Students' Disciplinary Board. Betty was shocked. Although that must have been obvious to her mother, the question was not withdrawn, however.

"Rumors," Mrs. Ellen Stone explained. "I've had a dozen telephone calls this afternoon. Mrs. Foley is very upset."

"Guilty, ma'am," Jimmy announced. "I don't know anything more, but I could tell by the expression on Betty's face when she came down the high school steps."

"Ridiculous!" Mrs. Stone said. Her hazel eyes flashed. All of her seemed to quiver with indignation. "How could you possibly decide they were guilty as charged, Betty?"

"The evidence was pretty overwhelming, I'm afraid. Jimmy, care to change into swim trunks? You go out through that glass door to that little shed on the other side of the patio. You'll find lots of swim trunks in there."

Jimmy left, taking his Seven-Up with him.

Betty looked at her mother, exasperated. "For goodness' sakes," she complained, "I'm not supposed to discuss Board business in front of students, Mom. Anyway, what does it matter to you?"

"Well, why should Mr. Swiftfoot's predicament matter to you? He's your friend, that's why. And Mrs. Foley and Mrs. Jorgenson are my friends. What happened at that meeting?"

Betty told her as quickly as she could, skipping nothing. Her mother's pretty, heavily tanned face was all scowls by the time she had finished. "Eloise Quayle, eh?" her mother said. "But why in the world was she so anxious to have a decision made in a hurry? Why did it seem important to her to get them convicted before you could conduct an investigation?"

"Because she was sure they were guilty, I

suppose. Anyhow, my conscience is clear. I voted no right to the bitter end. I was outvoted, and that's that."

"Did you think they were innocent?"

"Frankly, no. I just thought they should be given every chance to be proven innocent."

The ringing telephone interrupted the discussion. Betty started for the sliding glass door that connected the living room with the pool patio. Her mother ordered her to remain put, however. Her mother was gone for perhaps three minutes, and when she returned she was more upset than ever. "Mrs. Jorgenson," she said. "She got the news from Cora McHattie, and she's fighting mad. She claims that you kids convicted her son of cheating because you were jealous of his high grades. You know what else she said? She said that from now on we can take all our blacksmith work to someone else. She said that Mr. Jorgenson has shod the last Lightning W horse."

"Won't that hurt them more than us?"

"Of course! Why do you think I'm so upset? It always upsets me when people figuratively cut off their noses to spite their faces. Well, you run along to Jimmy. What a nice young man! Are you sure that he's real? I could hardly believe my eyes when I actually saw him bow over my hand. My goodness, perhaps he'll improve *your* manners."

"Not if he expects to marry me," Betty teased. "I'm a rootin', tootin' gal of the wild, wild West, and I intend to remain that way."

"With Mr. Swiftfoot's help, no doubt?"

Betty decided, chuckling, that she had given her mother enough news for one afternoon. She rushed up to her room and put on her black and tangerine bathing suit. Then she ran squealing to the swimming pool and told Jimmy that the last one in was a dope.

Already in the pool, Jimmy just laughed.

Chapter 3

On Sunday morning, at four o'clock, Betty got quietly from her bed and poked her head out of the dormer window to check the weather. It was quite cold, with a moistness in the air that suggested she would run into frost in the hill country. Betty dressed for the weather and a hard morning's work. Over her short-legged thermal union suit, she pulled heavy levi trousers and a checked flannel shirt and wool boot socks. She carried her boots downstairs and left them near the kitchen door. She made herself a hearty breakfast of three scrambled eggs, four slices of bacon, and a big bowl of instant oatmeal. She treated herself to three slices of toast with marmalade and two glasses of milk, to which she added generous measures of chocolate syrup. She ate slowly, thoughtfully, trying to plan so that her work would be performed efficiently. Actually, she anticipated little difficulty with the horses Mr. Swiftfoot had stolen. After all, they were pampered thoroughbred riding stock, not rough and tough mustangs accustomed to shifting for themselves on the range. In all probability, they would come for the first carrot she held out to them and would trot along quite happily back to their special pasture and comfortable stalls at the Lazy L Ranch. But she did anticipate considerable difficulty with Mr. Lucas. He was one adult she had never been able to understand. He could be very generous, as witness the money he gave to the school district each year to support the special classes in fine arts and music. But he could also be dirty mean, as witness the way he had tried to grab water holes to which he had no right until her father and some other ranchers had threatened him with the law.

As Betty saw it, much would depend upon luck. If the horses were returned to Mr. Lucas in good condition and if he happened to be in a good mood. Mr. Swiftfoot might well be given another chance. But what if luck were not with them this cold March morning in Arizona?

Betty sighed. Finished with her breakfast, she made some sandwiches and filled two canteens, then put on her boots and went across the yard to the barn. She took her lined denim chore coat from a hook and buttoned it up to the collar. She went out to the corral and whistled for Big Tom. All the horses stirred and several broke the morning quiet with loud whinnyings and snufflings. Big Tom came on the run and tried the old nonsense of looking for a carrot in one of her coat pockets. Betty laughed and swatted him affectionately and stood quite still until Big Tom's teeth had pulled the carrot out.

After he had gotten the carrot down the hatch, Big Tom was quite willing to be saddled and mounted. Indeed, he grew so impatient to be off through the starry early morning that he pawed the earth hard several times while Betty stowed things into the saddle bag and put on her Stetson and leather gloves. Once she was in the saddle, Big Tom moved fast. He did not let a little thing like a closed gate bother him. He went up and over the gate as if he had ridden steeplechase all his life. Big Tom came down running on the other side of the fence, and for well over a mile he thundered along in an abandoned sort of way as if intoxicated with the sheer joy of living. His joy infected Betty. Silly though it was, she threw her head back and yipped as the cowboys did when they were full of beans. Looking at the world shimmering in the starlight, feeling the cold air knifing cleanly down to her lungs, she suddenly wished she had nothing else to do all morning except ride where she chose. Some day soon, she promised herself, she would spend a Sunday morning that way. After the long year of school, it would be grand to forget studies for a while.

But she *did* have work to do now, she remembered, and it would be foolish to let Big Tom wear himself out before that work was accomplished. Hating to do it, Betty twitched the reins once, and Big Tom slowed to the easy canter he could maintain under even a broiling sun for a good five or six hours. After they had left Lightning W property, Betty eased him off in an easterly direction toward Big Camel Hills. It was her thought to reach Sheep Mesa before the sunrise began, and for a little while she thought she would make it. But Big Tom spotted a coyote in the lightening morning, and at once he began to behave with the silliness of a colt. He gave chase, and he would have worn the poor coyote out had Betty not finally pulled him in with all the strength at her command. Because of Big Tom's foolishness, the sun was up over the horizon when they finally reached Sheep Mesa, and they therefore missed the spectacle always made by the sun as it punctured the night with flame-gold spears of light that gradually broadened until all the eastern sky looked aflame.

Still, there was much beauty to see, particularly if you were an artist sensitive to every nuance of color, every effect worked by light and shadow. The sunrise red seemed to drip down the sky and stain the earth here and there. The stains spread in a quivering sort of way, making rocks and trees clear to the eye, exposing vast acres of range verdure. And onward marched the triumphant flood of sunlight, engulfing the night's purples and grays, transforming every drop of the night's dew into pinpoints of red and gold light. Suddenly full morning had come to the range. From Sheep Mesa Betty could see for miles in all directions; could see her family's ranchhouse so clearly it seemed only a few hundred yards away instead of about four miles. "Wave to Mom," she ordered Big Tom. "Brother, will we be scolded if we miss church!"

An antelope came bounding along, looking rumpled and wet after a night in the open. The antelope spotted them and stopped short. Betty called: "Well, sir, look at *you!*" Big Tom became jealous. Big Tom squealed, and he must have said something darned unfriendly, because the antelope raced off as if offended. Amused, Betty assured her big roan that she loved him very much indeed, and to prove it she dismounted to stretch her legs and give him a few minutes to investigate the terrain.

By nine o'clock they had reached Box Canyon deep in the tall, wooded hills. Betty had shucked her chore coat and gloves by then and shoved her Stetson far back on her honey-gold head. She was perspiring a bit and felt dusty and just a bit tired. She attributed her fatigue to the primarily indoor life she had necessarily led since the beginning of the school year in September. She became worried that the job of rounding up Mr. Lucas' horses might actually prove too much for her, so when they approached the canyon from the west she decided to do some reconnoitering. She got off Big Tom about a hundred feet from the canyon's brink. She walked quietly to the brink, then got down on her stomach and carefully looked down at the canyon floor. She was seen! There came to her ears the familiar sounds of a suddenly frightened horse. Three horses broke from cedar cover over near the creek at the far end of the canyon. They came hammering along the ground straight for the narrow canyon entrance, running so swiftly Betty had a vision of spending a full day trying to chase them down somewhere on the open range. But the leader halted just when it seemed he would lead the others to the wide open range. He tossed his head angrily, then whirled and went running back to the creek again. Exultant, Betty hustled back to Big Tom, and now she made full use of all his strength and speed and range savvy. She got him down the steep slope to the draw, clinging to him and yelling him on as he half ran and half slid in the general direction of the canyon entrance. She felt a bit ashamed of herself for having worked him so hard, though, after they had reached the entrance. There had been no reason for all that hurry! Naturally, Mr. Swiftfoot had blocked the entrance with rocks and limbs, thereby transforming the canyon into as tight a corral as anyone would wish. Grinning, Betty slipped on foot into the canyon itself and called to the Lucas horses. She had to call several times, but after that things worked out just fine. Three carrots and one lump of sugar to each horse convinced the thoroughbreds she was a friendly girl, easy to get along with. They permitted her to slip leather thongs around their necks and to tether them to a couple of trees. While she worked with Big Tom to pull the barrier down, the Lucas horses browsed as if content to be with a human being again. Nor were they at all fractious during the two-mile trip to the Lazy L. They kept to Big Tom's pace throughout and reached the ranch building in fine shape, not a one of them blowing or looking the worse for their experiences far from their comfortable stalls.

Betty was spotted riding in with the horses. A cowboy she knew gave her a big hello as she rode by one of the bunkhouses. He jumped up from the bunkhouse steps and took off his hat and kidded her. "Right nice ponies you got there, Miss Betty. You gonna sell them ponies to a poor cowboy that needs a new string? Give you a dime for the whole lot."

"Hi, Mr. Tomlin; your foreman around?"

The cowboy yelled for the foreman, and Mr. Burns came and said: "My, my, Christmas in March!" He gave the thoroughbreds

a practised examination and smiled broadly
with relief. "I'll say this for that Injun horse
thief," he said. "Wherever he put 'em, they
must have been real comfortable. Thoroughbreds are a finicky lot, Betty. If they don't
like a place or their feed, they thin down to
bones in a hurry. You better come palaver
with Mr. Lucas. Where'd you find them?"

"Oh, I just happened to spot them."

He understood that she had no intention
of answering any questions. Like all the
cowboys of Arizona, he respected her right
to keep her information to herself. "Well,"
he said mildly, "it's sure lucky you did spot
them. Horses like that we can sell for maybe
a thousand each."

"On our ranch, we give away better
horses than these," Betty teased him. "But I
will say this for your horses: they were very
cooperative."

Ten minutes later, the stolen horses back
in their special pasture, Betty was face to
face with the owner of the Lazy L Ranch.

Mr. Lucas greeted her with a big smile and a hearty handshake. "I'm certainly indebted to you, Betty," he said. "Those horses mean a lot to me. In fact, they're the only horses I seem able to ride around here. How did you happen to find them?"

Betty told him frankly, holding nothing back, letting him know right off exactly what she had told Mr. Swiftfoot in prison the day before. She had not gotten very far before the smile faded from Mr. Lucas' chubby red face. But she did not allow his altered expression to discourage her. She concluded: "I suppose you'll get the letter of apology tomorrow, Mr. Lucas. I think the apology will be sincere. After all, I'm sure Mr. Swiftfoot *is* sorry by now that he did something that caused him to spend a few days and nights in jail."

"In other words, you want me to let him off?"

Betty nodded.

Mr. Lucas shook his head. "No, sir. Everything turned out well, I'll admit that. Still, the horses could have been hurt or permanently lost. I think the best way to teach that Indian and any other potential horse thief a lesson is to let him spend at least a year in jail. Maybe when he's turned loose he'll have more respect for the property and rights of others."

Betty was shocked. "But he's an old man, sir! He needs special food, somebody to look after him. Anyway, I'll make him promise to behave, and he'll keep his promise to me."

"No, sir. I didn't get where I am by allowing anyone to take liberties with my property. That's that. Now let's talk about something more pleasant. You know that artist I've hired to paint that mural in my rumpus room? Well, he needs help. I want that mural finished by the end of June and he claims he can't make that deadline without help. All right. He says you do good painting, and I certainly owe you something for returning my horses. If you want a job,

I'll pay you a dollar an hour for working on that mural after school and on Saturdays and Sundays. What do you say?"

Betty was too confused to say anything. The change in the topic of conversation had been too abrupt. It was impossible for her to switch so quickly from thoughts of Mr. Swiftfoot to thoughts of art.

Fortunately, as it turned out, Mr. Lucas misunderstood. "Mad at me, eh? Think I'm a mean fellow, eh? Well, that's fine. You bet I'm mean! I never give something for nothing, and I never let people push me around. That's the only way I know to make a million dollars, and I have five million, more or less. All right. Now we understand each other, maybe we can do some business to make everyone happy. You do the work for free, and I'll give that old Indian a second chance he really doesn't deserve. Not to help the Indian, you understand, but to get something I want."

Betty's brown eyes shone. But the cowboys at the ranch had told her and even taught her the hard way never to grab any offer before she had done some serious thinking and hard bargaining.

"Actually," she told Mr. Lucas, "I should be paid a dollar an hour *plus* Mr. Swiftfoot's freedom. But I'll settle for seventy-five cents an hour if you let Mr. Swiftfoot come home with me today."

Mr. Lucas pointed to the door.

Betty started for the door, but she stopped short, because it occurred to her that she was not in a good position to bluff him as she had bluffed Mr. Swiftfoot yesterday afternoon.

"Fifty cents an hour, then?" she asked.

Mr. Lucas stood thinking a long time while Betty's heart seemed to fly to her throat and stay there.

At last Mr. Lucas nodded. "But you'd better work," he growled. "I'm a mean man who expects to get quality work for his money."

Chapter 4

Clara Greenley was frankly envious. A chubby, serious-minded girl who never failed to get A's or B's in any subject, Clara said on Tuesday afternoon: "I do wish I had your ability to get what you want. Do you know what some of the kids call you?"

"What?"

"Lucky Stone. Now I know and you know there's more than just luck involved in any triumph. Still, you do seem to score a lot more triumphs than anyone else."

"It was luck this time," Betty said soberly. "I don't think Mr. Lucas would have budged an inch if it hadn't been for that painting he wants. I tell you, he scared me, he really did, the way he looked when he said he doesn't allow anyone to take liberties with his property. I thought Mr. Swiftfoot would really sit in that old jailhouse for a year."

Their conversation in the waiting room was interrupted by Mrs. McCracken. The English II teacher and student supervisor for the month called from her office: "Come in, girls; please come in." After they had taken the chairs before Mrs. McCracken's desk, Mrs. McCracken held up a letter and said it contained the recommendation the Students' Board had made concerning Mary Foley and Ben Jorgenson.

"Girls," Mrs. McCracken continued, "I must tell you honestly that this recommendation displeased me. I have examined all the testimony that was submitted to the Board. All the evidence was hearsay evidence that proved nothing other than that our students are capable of making harsh judgments based on nothing more substantial than opinions."

Clara said quickly: "I'm not a member of the Board, Mrs. McCracken. You must have gotten my name by mistake."

"No mistake at all," Mrs. McCracken said cheerily. "You are here because you have an excellent mind and the ability to write reasonably acceptable prose. I propose to withhold action on this recommendation until the matter has been investigated thoroughly. Betty here will do the investigative work; you will write the report. I will *not* receive a report from any person who writes four lines and thinks she has said everything necesssary."

Betty had to laugh. She was still proud of the report to which Mrs. McCracken referred, even though it had earned her only a C. But she stopped laughing when she realized she would have to refuse the assignment to investigate the Foley-Jorgenson case. Under other circumstances she would have accepted the assignment gladly, if only to demonstrate to the guilty that the school faculty and student body were essentially fair people.

"I'm afraid I'll have to beg off," she told Mrs. McCracken. "I honestly hate to have to, but I'm sort of under contract to work for Mr. Lucas until the end of June."

"Contract? Your mother said nothing about such an obligation. Indeed, when I telephoned her a few minutes ago she was pleased that I had chosen you."

Betty felt a hot flush creep up to her hairline. She had to look out the window to avoid meeting Mrs. McCracken's china blue eyes. "Actually," she confessed, "I haven't told my folks about the job. It's a tricky situation, ma'am."

"It will be trickier, I suspect, if you don't tell them about it."

Clara explained: "Her folks don't like Mr. Lucas, ma'am. And her folks didn't exactly cheer when Betty brought Mr. Swiftfoot home with her from jail yesterday afternoon."

Mrs. McCracken tossed her gray head and said, "No wonder! It seems to me that every time I have two or three pies baked, that gluttonous man chooses to call on my husband. Still, none of this is solving the problem in hand. I could of course assign the investigation to someone else; Eloise Quayle, say. I doubt, however, that she would put her best efforts into it. Eloise would be scrupulously fair and honest, certainly, but she would not be enthusiastic."

"For instance," Betty said, to make her own position clear, "I have an appointment with Mr. Lockwood this afternoon, ma'am. I probably won't get home much before dinner."

Naturally, Mrs. McCracken was compelled to withdraw the assignment. Her manner suggested, however, a certain disappointment in Betty that troubled the girl after they had left the office. Betty looked directly into Clara's big green eyes. "Am I wrong," she asked, "or was Mrs. McCracken sort of displeased with me?"

Clara said too quickly, "How would I know?"

Her tone made Betty frown. She got the notion that Clara was also displeased with her, though why Clara should make a big deal out of the matter was more than she was able to figure out. She left Clara at the foot of the high school steps and walked on alone to Mr. Lockwood's art gallery and supply store on Bridle Street. She saw through the display window that he was busy with a couple of tourist ladies, so she walked on a couple of blocks more to the brick office building of the *Tincup Journal*. Mr. Bourke was busy writing at his desk, but he noticed her looking in at him and gave her a friendly wave to come inside. "What's new?" he asked as he always did. "I understand you entertained my newest reporter at your ranch Saturday evening. What do you think of him?"

"I like him."

He grinned. "What girl your age doesn't? It seems to me he's the most popular boy we've had around here in years. He's written a story about you, by the way. That's why I asked you to come in. Care to look at it?"

Betty was both thrilled and puzzled. "What could he possibly write about me?" she asked.

Mr. Bourke gave her the story and told her to read it for herself. It had already been set in type, she saw, and she could not help wondering what Mr. Bourke would do if she told him she did not want the story to appear.

The story was brief and well written. Right in the first sentence Jimmy announced the Miss Elizabeth Stone of the Lightning W Ranch had been chosen by Mr. Lucas to assist with the painting of a mural in the rumpus room of the new ranchhouse he was constructing on the Lazy L Ranch. Jimmy

then went on to say that many people in
Tincup considered Miss Stone to be the
most promising young artist in Arizona and
that Mr. Lockwood, the artist she would assist, had predicted when interviewed that
she would some day be as famous throughout the country as the great Western artist,
Frederick Remington, had been toward the
end of the last century.

Blushing, Betty put the story back onto
the desk. "It isn't true," she told Mr. Bourke.
"I don't have a chance of being a tenth as
good as Mr. Remington was. I don't see
things as truly as he did. I think Jimmy was
just trying to thank me for a nice afternoon
and evening at the ranch."

"The comment involving Remington was
obtained from Mr. Lockwood," Mr. Bourke
pointed out. "And I'll tell you something
else you ought to know. You know those little
pictures of desert flowers you did for your
church rummage sale last year? I bought
every one of them. Have them clustered on

either side of the fireplace in my living room. You'd be surprised if I told you how many friends of mine have tried to buy one or two from me. So don't be overly modest about your work. Sure, you have much to learn. That's natural. But you have a lot of talent, too. Want me to telephone your mother and read that story to her? I have a rule around here. I never print stories about minors without the approval of their parents."

Betty almost told him to go right ahead, please. It seemed to her to be a perfect way of letting her mother know about the job she had impulsively accepted Sunday morning. But almost in the same instant it occurred to her that that would be a coward's way of handling the matter. She shook her head. "Let me telephone her, if you don't mind. Ugh, the things I do so that stories written by my friends can be published! Mom will probably skin me a dozen different ways, starting from scratch."

She dialed the number and got her mother

after four or five rings. She said, "Hi, Mom," but that was as far as she could get for two minutes. Her mother gave her the same news Mrs. McCracken had given her, and her mother went on to say that she was proud a Stone had been given the important assignment to investigate the matter for the school. Betty glumly awaited her chance, and then told Mrs. Stone Jimmy Hayes had written a story about her that Mr. Bourke would print if he were given permission to do so.

"Wheeeee!" cried her mother. "Honey, what a privilege to know such a respected and famous girl. Read on, and don't leave out a single compliment."

Betty read the story in its entirety. When she had finished, she said quickly, "I didn't know how to break the news on Sunday, Mom. I was tired and all mixed up, and I had a lot on my mind."

"Have you actually agreed to work for that dreadful man? Have you pledged that you will help Mr. Lockwood?"

"Yes, ma'am."

Her mother asked coldly: "Then what can I do except authorize Mr. Bourke to print that story? Tell him to print it, please."

The next thing Betty knew, the connection was broken.

Sadly, she gave Mr. Bourke her mother's permission to print the story, and then she returned to Mr. Lockwood's shop and art gallery. He was just showing some tourist ladies out, each of them carrying Indian-made souvenirs of their visit to Tincup. Mr. Lockwood laughed and wagged his head after they had driven off. "The junk people buy!" he marveled. "Betty, you and I are in the wrong profession. We should manufacture junk; not try to paint quality pictures."

He led her through the cluttered shop to his studio in the rear. A small, quick-moving man with a pale face and a thick shock of glossy black hair, he took a batch of charcoal sketches from his desk and mounted them on an easel. "You're to help me with these," he said. "I'll rough in the broad outlines on the wall, and then you handle the details. The idea is to transform that wall into a spring desert covered with wild flowers."

Betty saw at once that she could handle her part of the assignment. For some reason, it had always been easy for her to paint flowers and plants that looked alive. She got into difficulty only when she tried to paint a human being, and since there would be no human beings in the mural, the whole thing would be as easy as riding for her. She nodded at Mr. Lockwood.

"Be sure of your colors and flowers," he warned. "That's the big problem in an assignment of this type. Mr. Lucas would not want a spring desert if he didn't know the spring desert. He'll spot just about every mistake you make."

And there would be many mistakes, Betty saw, if she used these sketches by Mr. Lockwood as models! Glory, she wondered, had

Mr. Lockwood never ridden to the desert to see with his own eyes exactly what saguaro cactus looked like when it was in bloom?

She asked very tactfully, "Would it be all right if I change these sketches as I paint? I'm not especially good at straight copying."

His black eyes danced. "Very nicely put," he told her. "But it's quite unnecessary to concern yourself about my feelings. An artist never objects to constructive criticism, especially when he knows that he knows little about the desert. You teach me to see desert flora as it is, and I'll teach you a few things you ought to know about composition. We both learn, we both make money, and we make a client happy. A perfect job and a perfect partnership, it seems to me."

For the first time, Betty became excited about the project. She put her things on a nearby chair and went to one of his work tables and got a fresh sheet of paper and a charcoal pencil. Working surely, forcefully, she sketched a saguaro cactus as she had seen one afternoon standing in solitary majesty on the brow of a small hill. But in the middle of the work she remembered her mother's reaction to the news of the job, and then the fun went out of everything.

Chapter 5

Mr. and Mrs. Gerald Stone of the Lightning W Ranch were industrious people possessed of a "live and let live" philosophy and a deep, abiding love for the outdoors. It was said by many in Tincup that the Stones would be the richest ranchers in Grand Valley if they were less generous with their money and less soft with the people who worked for them. But Jerry Stone refused to work his hired hands until they quit or dropped in their tracks, and Ellen Stone continued to make sizable contributions both to charitable organizations and to individuals who needed a helping hand. The result was that while the Stones were not the richest ranchers in the valley, they were among the most popular people in their section of Arizona. They never wanted for social invitations and they never wanted for all the hired hands they could use. Moreover, they had fun. Women were always dropping in to exchange recipes or discuss club projects with Ellen Stone. Men in all walks of life were always dropping by to discuss business or ranch or town problems with Jerry Stone over a sociable game of horseshoes. Almost everyone in town or on the range called the Stones a credit to the community, and it was significant that no matter how far Lightning W cattle or horses strayed from the ranch, they were sure to be brought back by someone.

Knowing all this, and knowing much more about the character of her parents than anyone else in Arizona, Betty was therefore puzzled and somewhat hurt when she was greeted coldly on her return home from Mr.

Lockwood's studio. Disturbed, she went straight to her room to change her clothes and wash and think. Although it was difficult for her ever to go where she felt she was unwanted, she got down to the kitchen at the customary time to help her mother with the last-minute dinner chores. Although she personally hated eggplant, she said to sweeten her mother's mood: "My, even the eggplant smells good. Did I tell you that we were given a lecture the other day about the importance of eating all vegetables? Mr. Swinton said—"

"Shush, dear. It will be all right after a while. Just give me time to remember that I was an impulsive, unthinking creature at your age, too."

Betty noticed Mr. Swiftfoot sitting under one of the cottonwood trees in the yard. It seemed to her that he had gained at least ten pounds since she had brought him back. It delighted her to see him looking so fat and clean and sassy and happy. "I can't keep quiet," she said. "Mom, I just love that man! I wish every girl in the world could grow up with a man like that around to show her desert flowers and teach her the way of desert creatures."

"He ate a whole apple pie this afternoon," her mother said coldly. "If I'd had a revolver handy, I think I'd have shot him dead. And then he actually had the nerve to say the pie wasn't nearly as tasty as some others I've baked."

Betty had to laugh, and once she had begun to laugh she just could not stop. She laughed until her sides ached and little tears were squeezed from her eyes. "What a tribute!" she sputtered. "Mom, aren't you proud he admires your cooking?"

"I am *not* proud," her mother said, "that you begged off from the assignment Mrs. McCracken gave you. I'm positive that if Mr. Swiftfoot needed your help again, you would find some way to help him."

Betty swallowed the last of her laughter.

She went to the dining room and set the table. Feeling insulted, she gave her mother the silence that had been requested, limiting her conversation to polite responses to questions and orders. After a time, at dinner, her father finally noticed that he was practically having a conversation with himself. He said: "Whoa, there!" and looked around the room and then under the table. "Strange," he said, "I thought I had a wife and daughter around. I must be going loco out here alone on the range."

Mrs. Stone told him to shush, too. Betty was shocked to the core. Never having seen her mother so disturbed, she developed a terribly guilty feeling deep inside her, and the next thing she knew she had to fight hard to keep tears from her eyes.

"Hey, girls," her father said, speaking very softly and tenderly now, "how about telling me the long tale of woe? We're supposed to love one another, remember?"

Betty asked if she could be excused.

"You may not be excused," her mother stated. Then, wonderfully, she smiled, smiled that big, soft, understanding smile that always left Betty feeling warm and secure and terribly wanted and even needed. "If anyone ought to leave this table," her mother continued, "it's I. I've broken the rules around here, haven't I? No grouchy people at table! All right. I apologize. Ice cream on the pie for dessert, even though a certain girl I know is beginning to look awfully hippy."

Betty said with a laugh that she was looking no such thing, and things were better after that. Her father was given all the news, with Betty filling in the details about which her mother knew nothing. He looked cross for a minute or so, but then a sudden thought put him in a better mood. "Well," he told Betty, "at least you didn't let the old man down. That's something. Loyalty counts for a lot with me."

Then Jerry Stone did something that surprised his daughter. For the first time in a year, he questioned her on her interest in making art her life's work. Some of the questions seemed strange to her, tending to be what the kids at school always classified as "typically juvenile adult questions." She answered each question as completely as she could, but when he suddenly asked why she was so convinced she simply had to be an artist, she had to laugh. "I just have to be," she told him. "Why do you have to be a rancher? Why does Mom have to be so interested in charity work and community projects? It's just the way you are, it seems to me. Clara Greenley and I have a theory about that. We think that every creature on earth is born to do certain things, that everything that happens in any creature's life is pre-ordained. A coyote is born to chase jackrabbits, a road-runner is born to scrap with rattlesnakes, you're born to operate this ranch, and so forth."

Mrs. Stone said, "That's an interesting

theory. And knowing the way your mind works, I suspect that you explain your talents as an artist in a manner entirely in accord with your theory."

"Well, after all," Betty argued, "I'd not be able to draw and paint if I'd been born to be a nurse, say. I wouldn't be interested in art if I'd been born to be a nurse."

"You expect to go to art school, then, after you've graduated?"

Betty met her father's eyes. "I'd love to," she said honestly. "I've dreamed of it more than once. I know it will cost a lot of money, at least in the beginning, until I've won some kind of scholarship. But Clara and I have a theory about that, too."

Her mother teased, "Such a lot of theories you moppets have."

Betty ignored the crack. "The theory is beginning to work out, too," she said triumphantly. "We were discussing it earlier this afternoon. Take my arrangemnt with Mr. Lucas. As I've figured it out, I'll earn approximately a hundred and forty dollars between now and the end of June. See? It's our theory that somehow, in some way, each of us will be able to earn enough money to pay for her education. It has to be that way, because if you're born to be an artist or a nurse you're darned well going to be what you were born to be."

Her parents exchanged glances, but it was difficult to tell in the candlelit room whether they were amused or impressed by her logic.

Jerry Stone took a pipe from the nearby rack and filled it and lighted up. He smoked for a time, busy with his thoughts, while her mother went to the kitchen to get the promised pie à la mode. Nothing more was said on the subject of art until after dessert had been eaten and the dinner things washed and put away. Then, as Betty was going upstairs to her room to tackle her homework, her father called to her from his little office off the living room. When she went inside she found him at his desk, looking thoughtfully at a little stack of mail. He grinned, rose, seated her, and aimed a mock punch at her little chin. "Don't look so scared," he ordered. "Just between you and me, I'm glad to have Mr. Swiftfoot back with us. He has a nice hand with chickens and horses. No, this is a different matter. The reason I asked all those questions about your interest in art is this: I could use a hostess for our dude ranch this summer. Or your mother could, since she really runs it. We were thinking about looking around for some girl your age to handle the job; some girl who really knows horses and the country and has a strong sense of responsibility. Well, at the dinner table it suddenly occurred to me that you are the girl I'm looking for. If you saved the salary, you'd have some extra money when you go away to art school."

Betty's heart began to thump. She looked at her father's tanned, boyishly handsome face and wondered suddenly why she was ever cross with him or rude to him or resentful when he exercised his parental authority. He always seemed to understand her! He always seemed willing to recognize she was a person, entitled to dream her own dreams, to make her own mistakes, to do her best on her own to cope with life.

"Want to consider it?" he asked. "A hundred a month and room and board. You can handle the work, I know, because you handled the problem of Mr. Swiftfoot."

Betty said from her heart: "Dad, you've just hired a hostess! Wheee, let's tell Mom!"

Chapter 6

Throughout April and May, Betty was among the busiest and happiest girls in the vicinity of Tincup, Arizona. For the first two weeks after she had begun to assist Mr. Lockwood, she had Jimmy Hayes drive her to the studio directly after school for three hours of preliminary sketching. Then, when she felt actual work on the mural was justified, she drove out to the Lazy L Ranch with Mr. Lockwood each week day afternoon to transfer her sketches to the wall of the spacious rumpus room of the unfinished ranchhouse. In no time at all she was on very friendly terms with the carpenters and other people who were building the elegant house for Mr. Lucas. Frequently men found some excuse or other to come into the room and watch her work. These were not men who were easily pleased. Most of them had grown up in that particular section of Arizona and therefore knew the desert plants and flowers as well as she. If she did not get the spines of a cactus just so, they were mighty quick to tell her. One afternoon, indeed, she got little work done because of a lengthy debate on the subject of how she had presented a clump of ocotillo. Even Mr. Lucas joined in the debate, growling and sputtering and pretending to be all upset but actually having a fine time. In the end, when Betty had proved to everyone's satisfaction that she really knew exactly how ocotillo looked in bloom, Mr. Lucas suggested to the men that they do the carpentry and allow "this sassy kid" here to do the mural painting. Later, while she was waiting outdoors for one of her father's cowboys to come for her in the jeep, Mr. Lucas asked her how she had been able to learn so much about the desert in so short a period of time. She told him about the trips she had often made into the desert with Mr. Swiftfoot. He said wistfully that he wished he had been with them on some of those trips, and he then suggested that perhaps one day soon they all ought to ride to the desert for a good look around while everything was in bloom.

The upshot of this conversation was that the three of them did make half a dozen trips to the desert, and these outings were useful to Betty in more ways than one. Apart from the fact that they made nice breaks in the routine of school work and mural painting, they provided her with fresh information she was able to incorporate into her work for Mr. Lucas as well as into her planning of the summer's activities at the dude ranch. On the last of the trips, indeed, it occurred to her that the city kids who would spend the summer at the dude ranch would find it darned exciting actually to camp on the desert for a few days. She went home excitedly late that day to discuss the idea with Mr. McWilliams, her father's foreman. Mr. McWilliams gave the idea deep consideration and then nodded. "Ought to be fun, girl," he said. "Of course, it's hot as blazes on the desert, but if you got up in the hills on the edge of the desert, you could ride out to the desert in the evening cool. I could spare some fellows to prepare a camping place, I guess."

"Why not two cowboys for the whole summer, Mr. McWilliams? They're not too awfully busy at that time of year."

He said he would think it over, and he must have seen it her way, because a few days later her mother asked at breakfast: "Honey, have you been sweet-talking our Mr. McWilliams? He came to your father yesterday and offered to assign two cowboys and three field hands to our dude ranch this summer. I was never so surprised in my life. Every year except this one I've had to battle him for the men I thought I needed."

Betty asked: "Are you in the habit of going to him for his opinion, Mom? I've always found that Mr. McWilliams is most helpful if you tell him your problem and ask him for his opinion. But if you just go to him with decisions or orders—well, he doesn't like that. After all, he's an important man, isn't he? A foreman is a pretty important man in these parts."

Her mother gave her a strange look. "Why, for goodness' sakes," her mother exclaimed, "I think you've cleared up the mystery of his opposition to me! It's quite probable I've been less impressed by his position than I ought to have been. Drat. I'm afraid my Eastern background betrayed me. To me, Mr. McWilliams has always been just a hired hand. But he's actually an executive, of course. Well! Do I bake him a chocolate cake or what to tell him I'm sorry?"

Betty felt uncomfortable, as she invariably did when her mother asked her advice. "I guess you know more about that sort of thing than I," she finally mumbled. "If there's one thing you Easterners know darned well, it's manners and entertaining and such. Do you ever miss the East, Mom? Do you ever hone to be a schoolteacher again?"

"Not really. I'm a doer, not a rememberer. Oh, I suppose I do think of the East at times, especially when I've received a letter from your Aunt Mary. And that's comical, in a way, because Chicago doesn't seem like the East to Easterners, as it does to us out here."

In the end, a chocolate cake was made for Mr. McWilliams and Betty went with her mother to deliver it to him that evening in his cottage among the cottonwoods near the creek. In a sense, the delivery of the cake at that particular time was most unfortunate, for there in the pretty front yard with Mr. McWilliams was old Mr. Swiftfoot himself. One sniff of the cake caused Mr. Swift-foot's beak of a nose to wiggle. "Excellent," Mr. Swiftfoot said. "Chocolate cake pleases me."

Mr. McWilliams stood up, red of face and somewhat nervous. He grew redder and more nervous when Ellen Stone told him clearly that the cake was her way of apologizing to him for having sometimes forgotten they all owed much of the prosperity of the Lightning W Ranch to his savvy and efforts. "Hey," Mr. McWilliams rumbled, deeply embarrassed, "all I do is my job." Still, he accepted the cake and politely invited them to share it with him. Betty and her mother as politely told him they could not eat so much as a crumb. Old Mr. Swift-foot was less polite. "More for us," he said greedily. "Let's eat!"

From that moment on, Mr. McWilliams' long opposition to the operation of a summer dude ranch for youngsters was just a memory. Every minute of the time that

Betty could spare from her art and studies and chores was claimed by the foreman and was usually spent at the north end of the property, where the dude ranch was located. They inspected the bunkhouses and they inspected the recreation building and they inspected the chuckhouse. Mr. McWilliams found just about a million things in need of repair or other attention. He also decided that the location of the corral ought to be changed. "Horses like more privacy," he told her one evening; "at least our cow ponies do. What we ought to do is set the corral up there in the hills a way. That way, they're screened by the trees, get a natural spring to drink from, have sunshine or shade as they wish."

"Maybe the kids won't want to walk so far," Betty said dubiously.

"Do 'em good! Now you take some advice from me, young lady. This being hostess on a dude ranch isn't exactly easy work. You get maybe fifty or sixty kids to keep happy, you have a problem. They have more energy than a roadrunner battling a rattlesnake. One way to work the energy out of them is to give them a lot of walking to do."

That seemed logical to Betty. "Wonderful, Mr. McWilliams! When do you want me to help you?"

"Hey, that's man's work. Anyhow, it seems to me you're pretty busy these days. You let me talk it over with your folks and then handle it for you."

So it went throughout the busiest and happiest eight weeks Betty had ever known. Problems came up but were solved. Mistakes were made but corrected. Plans were made and were changed. And bit by bit things were accomplished, good things that gave her every reason to believe that the busyness was worth-while.

Then, abruptly, two things happened that changed everything. One afternoon at the school, Clara's brother Billy announced casually that Mary Foley and Ben Jorgenson had finally taken tests in a desperate attempt to prove their high grades since the first of the year had been earned through honest study and not contemptible cheating. And this time, Billy said, both Mary and Ben had scored A's despite the fact they could not possibly have known anything whatsoever about the types of questions that would be asked. While all the kids sat marveling about that, Billy looked at Betty and said harshly: "I blame you, Miss Self-Centered. I don't blame Eloise or anyone else on the Board; just you. And do you know why? Because you didn't believe they were guilty in the first place; because you might have proven they weren't guilty if you hadn't washed your hands of them.

Betty gazed at him mutely, feeling so ill all of a sudden that she wanted to get up and run.

"Boy," Billy raged on, "what a classic example of selfishness! It didn't matter to you that they needed the help of the one person who believed in them. All you were interested in was earning money, getting your name in the newspaper, making like a business girl on the ranch."

His violent tone frightened Betty, and she gathered her legs up under her to rise and leave.

Strangely enough, however, Eloise Quayle came to her defense. Eloise said in her usual positive tone, "Your devotion to Mary Foley is touching, Billy, but your words do you little credit. The fact is that you betray the typical stupidity of boys. Betty here never doubted they were guilty. Her argument was simply that we ought to leave no stone unturned to get every fact possible before we made the recommendation that was made. She spoke and then I spoke and then we voted. She was outvoted. She accepted the opinion of the majority, as you're supposed to do if the democratic process is to mean anything. Instead of kicking up a big storm that might shatter the confidence of the kids in the Students' Disciplinary Board, she kept quiet and withdrew from the case. It wasn't a matter of selfishness. She simply accepted the decision of the majority."

"Just don't run for any class office next year," Billy said to Betty. "I'll campaign against you."

Betty left them, thinking that if she did not there would be a real brawl right there on school grounds. Perhaps she *had* been too concerned with her own affairs.

That evening, as she always did when troubled, she put the question to her mother as they were doing the dishes after dinner. "It's possisble you have been concentrating on yourself," her mother said carefully. "That's natural, at your age. To most people in their middle teens, the world seems to begin and end with themselves. But you must be fair to yourself, too. After all, you did become involved with the mural because you were concerned about that Indian who will some day eat us out of house and home. I think you ought to have a chat with Billy when he's had a chance to cool off. Explain to him frankly exactly how you got the job with Mr. Lucas. I'd be sorry if you and Billy became enemies. I've always liked Billy and Clara and all the other Greenley children."

"But it is true," Betty said gloomily, "that I didn't really care what happened to Mary and Ben. That was certainly an antisocial attitude."

"Well, never you mind. I love you, your father loves you, Mr. Swiftfoot loves you, and even Aunt Mary loves you. Oh, that reminds me. Aunt Mary showed one of your paintings to her employer, Mr. Gifford. Mr. Gifford in turn showed it to an art critic he knows in Chicago. The upshot of it all is that Mr. Gifford will pay for art lessons with a famous teacher in Chicago if you can coax us into letting you live there for a year."

It seemed so fantastic to Betty that she did not believe the story for even a moment.

"Good old Mom," she said, beginning to feel less gloomy. "I can always depend upon you to give my morale a boost. But such whoppers you tell! Aren't you ever ashamed?"

"Aunt Mary's letter is on my bureau," her mother said. "Of course, the proposition is ridiculous and you won't be going to Chicago, but it may interest you to see the proof that she adores you as we do."

Betty inhaled sharply and raced upstairs for the letter.

Chapter 7

From the moment she read Aunt Mary's letter, Betty's delight with her life in Arizona went winging. Had she been given any say in the matter, she would have packed her clothes that same evening and left by bus the next morning for Chicago. Room! Board! Art lessons! Museums! Daily association with her favorite aunt in one of the great, storied cities of America! In short, Aunt Mary offered in her letter practically everything Betty had ever dreamed while she had sat alone on the range painting and painting and painting to improve her technique. After she had read the letter at least a dozen times, Betty went to her room and threw herself ecstatically onto her bed. She never doubted that her folks would allow her to leave. She gave not a thought to the fact that she had hired out to Mr. Lucas until the end of June and had also hired out to her parents until the close of the dude ranch season in mid-September. Staring at the silvered, combed-plywood ceiling, Betty gave serious thought to the type of art lessons she wanted. She finally decided that she would ask her teacher to stress composition. Thanks to the training in observation that Mr. Swiftfoot had given her, she could handle details easily, almost without thought. But the arrangement of those details into a composition at once bold and unified was a skill she had not yet acquired. So at first the emphasis would have to be placed upon composition. Then—

A knock on the door broke off her thoughts.

She called for her father to come in, sat

up and tugged the hem of her skirt down over her knees. She regarded him with dancing eyes as he sank into the blue naugahyde armchair her folks had given her at Christmas. "Fine friend," she twitted him. "You could have hinted about that letter at dinner. That way I wouldn't have been so surprised."

"Well, you weren't at dinner, exactly. Your body was there, but not your mind. I understand some of the kids gave you a rough time."

"Oh, Billy was just talking, I think. He's pretty fond of Mary Foley. That's interesting, by the way. Last year at this time Billy could think about nothing except baseball and cattle and such. Whenever a girl showed up, Billy always had something caustic to say. Now it's just about the other way around. Isn't that odd?"

"Oh, I don't know," Jerry Stone said easily. "A person's interests change as he grows up. It seems to me that yours have been changing, too. I hear talk now and then that you see a lot of Jimmy Hayes."

"You bet! Do you know why? Because a girl can talk to him seriously and be taken seriously. So many of the boys are plain silly. All this mush and slush they talk, it's downright disgraceful. Do you know what one of the boys did the other day? He sent me a five-page poem entitled, 'My Lady of the Sage.' It was a direct steal, too, from Tennyson's *The Lady of Shalott*."

Because her father looked a trifle skeptical, Betty recited:

"On either side the desert lie
  Stone hills that batter at the sky. . . ."

She laughed. "You see? That's how ridiculous most of the boys are these days. Glory, did some of the girls laugh when I read it to them."

He scowled. "I don't think that was very nice, honey. Speaking from experience, a fellow puts a lot of work and his heart into writing a poem to a girl. Anyway, those are private matters."

"Jimmy is never that silly," Betty said. "I don't like people to be silly."

Her father shrugged, then reached out for the letter on Betty's night table. He looked at the letter for two or three minutes, his brows drawn together, his expression a bit sterner than Betty liked. Betty misunderstood. "Well," she offered, "I'll apologize to the boy, if you think I should. I wasn't trying to be mean. It just struck me as being sort of funny. I don't think I've ever been out with that boy alone in my life. And then to get a poem like that!"

"You see a lot of Jimmy, though. Think that's a good idea, at your age? It seems to me that a girl your age should be growing in all ways, learning from experience as well as books. This business of limiting your social life to just one fellow and maybe four or five girls doesn't strike me as being too smart."

"Actually, it's more business than social

with Jimmy," Betty told him thoughtfully.
"I've never met a person like Jimmy before.
He's strictly business. He eats and breathes
and sleeps newspaper stuff. Lots of times,
he practises on me . . . you know, asking
questions and things like that. It works out
very well. He shows me some things before
he shows them to Mr. Bourke. And I show
him sketches sometimes before I show them
to Mr. Lockwood or Mr. Lucas. We have a
pact to be entirely honest with each other.
If I don't like a story, I tell him so, and if
he doesn't like a sketch, he tells me so. Of
course, we do get into some real discussions
at times over cokes in Pop Reardon's drugstore. Pop laughs and laughs. But we profit
from those discussions all right."

"My, you never flounce out? You must be
growing up."

Betty was indignant. "Dad," she said icily,
"I *am* almost sixteen. And according to some
things I've been reading, a girl is pretty mature at my age, a lot more mature than most

fellows."

Somewhere outside, a coyote began to yelp. Reminded that time was passing, Betty stood up and went to the closet for her denim outdoor clothes. "I'm riding to the dude ranch," she said. "Care to come along? If Mr. McWilliams hasn't painted those bunkhouses the colors I suggested, there'll be a shooting match."

"Yellow with brown trim. I almost fell out of the saddle, but he told me he was just following your instructions. Think you'll really love that yellow all the long summer through?"

Betty chuckled. "Won't have to stand it now," she announced exuberantly. "Dad, isn't it wonderful how things work out? I never dreamed Aunt Mary would show that painting to her boss. She just wanted it, so I gave it to her. And here I am, going to Chicago for a year, all because of that painting!"

His frown made his face sterner than

ever. Betty was puzzled, because generally he looked so stern only when he had something unpleasant to say or do. "Hey," she rebuked him, "folks aren't supposed to scowl so in this house. Ask Mom!"

He did not laugh. He simply asked: "But what about your job this summer, honey? We had a talk about your future around March, and we decided you'd be hostess on the dude ranch for wages. How come you think you're free now to accept Aunt Mary's offer?"

Betty looked at him incredulously. She stammered, "But—but a chance like this—"

"Slow down," he ordered. "How can we discuss it intelligently with you sputtering around here like a firecracker? Hang it, though, there's my point. Do you have any idea of what it would cost everyone to give you that year in Chicago? Those lessons would cost Mr. Gifford about five hundred dollars. Add the cost of your room and board. Add all those extra costs girls your age rack up without even realizing it. As I figure it, it would come close to our thousand dollars. And all for what? How do I know you're any more serious about art than you are about other things?"

"But of course I'm serious!"

"Maybe so, maybe not. Here's what I mean. Last October when you were elected to the Students' Disciplinary Board, you told me it was a great honor and that you wouldn't ever let the school or the kids down. But you forgot that promise the first time you were asked to do extra work investigating that cheating matter."

"How could I do it, Dad? I was trying to help Mr. Swiftfoot."

"Really? You had the time to do extra work on the dude ranch, I notice. When it was something you wanted to do, you found the time, all right."

Betty felt her cheeks tingle. She knew suddenly that this was what Billy had meant when he had called her self-centered. She sat down weakly on the bed, her fingers toying with her skirt.

"And now," Jerry Stone said grimly, "you're ready to turn your back on the dude ranch because something more exciting has come along. All of a sudden the work you were seriously interested in has no meaning whatsoever for you. You see what I mean, honey? What's in your record this year to convince your mother and me that you're really serious about anything? How do we know that you wouldn't drop your lessons in Chicago the instant something more exciting came along?"

Betty felt tears gathering in her eyes. His voice, his manner, the way he was looking at her, made her feel terribly juvenile and silly and somehow dreadfully in the wrong. She said intensely, "It means so much to me, Dad; really it does." But she might as well have spoken to one of the pine-paneled walls.

"To me," Jerry Stone said, "the difference

between a young woman and a girl is the difference between accepting and junking responsibility. To me, words mean little. Anyone can speak words, make promises. What counts with me is action, measuring up to the responsibilities one accepts. I'm afraid the answer has to be no, honey. My conscience wouldn't let me allow this Mr. Gifford and your Aunt Mary to spend good money on you until I was sure you were serious enough to work, to stick it out until the finish, come what might."

He stood up and took a step toward the door. Aware that her big chance was slipping from her grasp, Betty called out frantically, "But I *am* serious this time, Dad, truly I am!"

He swung around to face her, tall and slim and very handsome in his pearl gray rancher's trousers and dark blue shirt with silver buttons. But he did not come forward to take her in his arms as he used to years ago whenever she was troubled. Instead he snapped, "You'll have to prove it to me, young lady. The opportunity you want is an opportunity for responsible adolescents, not irresponsible kids. All right. Handle your responsibilities this summer, and we'll take a good look at the subject in the fall."

He left then, moving so quickly there was no time for Betty to argue with him.

Betty chewed on her lower lip, telling herself sternly that she would not cry, that tears were for babies, not for girls almost sixteen. But the tears came anyway, and she thought childishly, rebelliously: I hate him! I'll go to Chicago anyway!

Chapter 8

Because of the disapproving attitudes of many of the kids and her father, Betty found June to be the unhappiest month she had ever experienced. She hated to go to school; she hated to spend an unnecessary minute at home. What she really wanted to do, she told herself several times, was to sneak aboard one of the freight trains that stopped in Tincup and hitch a ride across the Rocky Mountains and the plains to Chicago. One afternoon she actually went to the freight depot, fully determined to sneak into the first empty box car she saw. She never climbed into one, however. It occurred to

her that if she did she would make a great
deal of difficulty for everyone and convince
everyone that she just could not stand up to
disappointment. Scowling, she turned on
her heel and left the depot area as quickly
as she could. She went to the studio, put on
her smock, and sat down on the stool before
the drawing bench Mr. Lockwood had
turned over to her. She worked so industri-
ously for ten or fifteen minutes that Mr.
Lockwood finally looked up from a photo-
graph he was retouching to say: "No need
to wear yourself out now, Betty. That's the
last sketch. Even if we loaf a bit, we'll finish
that mural a week ahead of time."

"I'll be sorry to finish the mural," Betty
confessed. "This has been wonderful for me,
Mr. Lockwood."

His black eyes twinkled. "Well, you aren't
going to leave town, are you?" he asked.
"You're always welcome to drop in. And
who knows, perhaps I'll have assignments to
give you from time to time. I'll tell you what.

Why don't you exhibit some of your desert paintings here? I'm sure we can sell a few for you this summer. Tourists are always interested in buying souvenirs if they're not too expensive."

Any other time, Betty would have been thrilled. It was definitely a tribute to her work. Now, however, her mood was such that nothing thrilled her these days. "If you like," she agreed politely.

A few days later, when she had to say something at the dinner table to avoid being called a "silly sulk," Betty told her mother about the invitation to exhibit her work in Mr. Lockwood's art gallery. Her mother was so surprised she almost dropped the vegetable dish she was passing to Betty's father. "Really?" her mother asked. "How wonderful! What have you decided to exhibit there?"

Betty admitted she had not given the matter the consideration it deserved. Her mother said that she was scandalized. Directly after dinner, they went out to the barn and climbed to the hayloft to poke around in the little room Betty used as a studio. There were fully a hundred canvases there, neatly arranged in the racks one of the cowboys had built to keep them off the floor. Betty's mother sat down and began to take the paintings out and look them over critically. But she was no help at all, Betty discovered quickly. To her mother, everything signed "Betty S" was perfect. At any other time, Betty would have accused her of judging art with her heart rather than with her mind. Now, however, with her own heart so heavy, she simply told her mother that the most Mr. Lockwood would want would be five paintings, if that. "Well, then," her mother said, "you'll just have to give him *Desert Twilight*. Really, Rabbit, I think that is a fine painting. The sage looks so beautifully mysterious in the twilight I get a lump in my throat each time I see it. And *Lonesome Butte!* You must give him that one, too."

Betty said it really made no difference what was exhibited at the gallery.

At that point, her mother said: "Whoa!"

Their eyes locked.

Mrs. Stone did something she had not done in years. She pulled her daughter down to her lap, smoothed the girl's honey-gold hair and kissed the damp forehead. "Let's powwow," Ellen Stone said. "Let's assume for the time being, at least, that the Rabbit is a woman and that I can talk to her as woman to woman. All right?"

"Mom, I'll squash you! I'm a tub these days."

"Nonsense. Mere youth fat. A good summer on the range will burn the old lard off in a hurry. But to talk as woman to woman: how long will the sulks last? I never have approved of sulks."

"I'm sorry."

"Now, now, no fibs. You're not a bit sorry. As a matter of fact, you're rather pleased in a perverse sort of way that your father is unhappy. You'll show him, eh? Next time he'll know better than to disappoint you! My, what a fine woman we have here!"

"I can't pretend!" Betty said hotly. "I'm not a piece of stone; I'm a human being! Naturally I'm unhappy. Wouldn't you be unhappy if someone arbitrarily said you couldn't have the schooling you thought you needed?"

"Doubtless I'd be unhappy. But I think I'd be inclined to believe the decision wasn't necessarily made to cause me unhappiness."

"Dad just doesn't understand! Mom, this is vital to me."

"No. First things first. Painting is for mature people. First you mature; then you acquire the instruction only the mature can use effectively. To be honest, I rather admire the lord and master for the firmness he has shown. I support his decision to the full."

"Oh, that's fine; that's wonderful!"

"Believe it or not, honey," and now Ellen Stone's voice was soft and wonderfully musical, "you'll be grateful to us one of these days. In the meantime, do you stop sulking and rejoin the human race, or do we kick you out to join all the grumpy coyotes on the range?"

Betty stared.

"Well, not exactly the range," her mother hedged. "But if you're unhappy with us and we're unhappy with you, we could make things easier for everyone by shifting you to one of the bunkhouses on the dude ranch. You'll be living there this summer anyway, of course."

To Betty, that was definitely the last straw. She sprang to her feet. "I'll move at once," she said.

She flounced off to one of the bunkhouses and called imperiously to Mr. Swiftfoot. When the old Indian came out, smiling, she told him that she had been kicked out of her own home and needed help getting her things shifted to the girls' bunkhouse on the dude ranch. The work took the better part of two hours. At the end, they were assisted by Mr. McWilliams himself, and after Betty had put her things away to her liking in her private room in the bunkhouse, the foreman told Mr. Swiftfoot that he was now officially on the payroll to act as bodyguard and general assistant to the "spitfire." Mr. Swiftfoot nodded and began to swagger around. "I like money," he said with engaging frankness. "I like the feel of money in my pocket."

The two men went off somewhere to discuss the wages Mr. Swiftfoot would be paid. The salary must have been satisfactory to the old Indian. In the morning, when Betty stepped outdoors, she saw smoke pluming from the chuckhouse smokestack across the way from the bunkhouse. When she went into the chuckhouse she found Mr. Swiftfoot busy at the stove. "Golden Hair," he said contentedly, "go back and take your bath. Are you an Indian? Only an old Indian lives without baths."

"I'm hungry," Betty said. "My, look at you work! But don't ever let Mom see you, or you'll cook for us and all the hands."

"You like your eggs sunny side up?"

"Scrambled."

"This morning you eat them sunny side up."

Chuckling, Betty ate them sunny side up. At the usual time she went to the house to get the usual lift to the Greenleys' Tomahawk Ranch and the school bus. Her father came out, said, "Hi," and led her to the jeep. If he was sorry about anything, his expression did not reveal it. "The first gang of kids will be coming on July first," he announced. "Ten girls, fourteen boys. I've hired Billy Greenley to help with the boys. Next week we'll have a chat and work out the routine for the summer. Meanwhile, why don't you get the Lucas painting out of the way and have some fun?"

"Is that an order, sir?" Betty asked petulantly.

His jaws tightened, but that was his only reaction to her freshness. "Suit yourself," he said mildly, and that was the last thing he did say during the ride.

Chapter 9

The day before the Lightning W Dude Ranch opened for the season, Billy Greenley rode in on Thunder, his favorite bay gelding. For the occasion Billy wore elegant gray riding pants, a violet shirt, a black and yellow neckerchief and a gray Stetson with the widest brim any cowboy on the Lightning W had ever seen. Billy also wore chaps and new boots. His spurs jingled every time Thunder took a step, and it was this jingling of spurs that brought out the mischief in the cowboys. "Son," one drawled, "I ain't heard purtier music since I left Texas. Play me a tune, son; play me a pretty cowboy tune."

Billy reddened somewhat while the cowboys gathered around and marveled at the beauty of his outfit. But when one of the cowboys stopped marveling and made a comical remark about the dude rider and his dude horse, Billy could contain his anger no longer. "If anybody thinks Thunder is a dude horse," Billy challenged, "let's have a race."

There were whoops of delight, for there was nothing that pleased the men more than a race on the open range. At least ten of the Lightning W cowboys went to the corral to saddle their favorite ponies. While they were busy, Mr. McWilliams decided that it ought to be a real test of horse flesh and indicated a three-mile course by pointing first to Sentinel Rock, then to the cottonwoods along Mary's Creek, then to a line he drew with his boot from the corral fence to the fence of Ellen Stone's kitchen garden. Mr. McWilliams borrowed a Colt .38 from one of the cowboys and fired a shot into the air to start the race. Before the cowboys quite appreciated what was happening, Thunder shot off to a ten-yard lead and went streaking across the range toward Sentinel Rock. The moment Betty saw that, she wagged her head at Mr. McWilliams. "There goes the horse race," she said. "Big Tom might catch Thunder, but not any of the horses our cowboys are riding."

"Girl," he rebuked, "never sell a mustang short. They have lots of grit and stamina."

But the race ended just as Betty had thought it would. While it was true that none of the mustangs quit, it was also true that none seriously challenged Thunder for the lead. Actually, Billy was pulling the gelding in hard when Thunder crossed the finish line a good fifteen lengths ahead of the nearest horse. Billy then had a fine time razzing the riders as they came in one by one. "Boys," Billy asked, "where'd you ever get those coyotes you call horses? And talk about amateur riders! Over on the

Tomahawk Ranch, the girls ride better than you do."

And whistling, his head high, his back ramrod straight, Billy eased Thunder around the Stone ranchhouse and headed for the dude ranch in the distance. Betty wheeled Big Tom around and went after Billy. When she had caught up with him, she congratulated him on his victory. She did more. Quickly, she took the action she had planned the moment she had learned Billy would spend the summer as an employee of the dude ranch. "And while we're talking of riding," she went on, "we may as well get something settled here and now. To me, this is purely a business relationship. If you do your work properly, I won't bother you. Naturally, I'd rather have some other boy here, just as you would rather have some other girl. But I won't spend the summer arguing with you. Fair enough?"

"Suits me," Billy said shortly. He reined Thunder in when he saw the bright yellow bunkhouses and chuckhouse. "Now I've seen everything," he commented. "All you have to do is paint the corral rails a pretty pink. Say, where is the corral?"

Betty told him it had been shifted into the hills on the recommendation of Mr. McWilliams. Billy was interested not so much in this news as he was in the implication that Mr. McWilliams was deigning to notice the dude ranch this year. "What did you do," Billy asked: "charm him as you charmed Mr. Lockwood and Mr. Lucas?"

"Oh, I'm just a regular charmer," Betty said. "I may be self-centered, but I do charm anyone I want to charm." She jiggled the reins, and Big Tom loped ahead. In front of the chuckhouse she dismounted and turned Big Tom over to Manuel, one of the field hands Mr. McWilliams had assigned to the dude ranch. Then she went to the chuckhouse to check the progress in there. She found Mr. Swiftfoot hard at work shifting cans of things from cartons to storeroom shelves. Supervising his work, but giving him much physical assistance, too, was none other than Mrs. Kathy Foley. Betty tried to conceal her surprise, but was clearly unsuccessful. "Hi," Mrs. Foley said. "I'm no more surprised than you, young lady. But your mother telephoned she wanted me again this year, so here I am."

"Glad to have you," Betty said politely. But she went back outdoors as quickly as she could to do some serious thinking about the fact that her mother had employed for the season two helpers who certainly had no reason to adore Miss Betty Stone of the Lightning W Ranch. She wondered what her mother was trying to accomplish.

It was while she was pondering the matter that the first customer of the season arrived. A duo-toned horn beeped once, and there was a chauffeured limousine gliding to a halt about ten feet from her. A girl her age poked a beautifully coiffured head out the rear window of the limousine and called: "Miss, can you tell us where the Lightning W Dude Ranch is?"

"Right here, believe it or not."

The girl frowned. "Now, really," she protested, "you don't call *this* a ranch. Where are the cattle, the romantic cowboys?"

Betty chuckled and opened the rear door. "Oh, we have them," she assured the girl. "I'm Betty Stone, by the way, official hostess and unofficial ramrod of this outfit."

The girl started to take Betty's proffered hand, but changed her mind. She explained: "Germs, you know. One can never be too careful about germs."

She got out of the limousine, looked around in disapproving fashion and demanded to see the bunkhouse for girls. Betty led her into the bunkhouse and gestured toward the double-bunk beds. "Nothing fancy," she said unnecessarily. "You stow your gear in a locker; you stow your valuables at the house."

The girl looked positively appalled. "Are

you insinuating that I'm to share quarters with thirty girls? But that's preposterous! I wouldn't think of doing so!"

With an effort, Betty managed a smile. "Well," she said, "I don't know where else you can stay, Miss—"

"Robbins, Elaine Robbins."

Betty remembered the name. The request for a reservation for a full summer for Miss Elaine Robbins had come five weeks ago from some place in distant Delaware.

Betty decided that the matter would have to be settled by her mother. She went into her private room and worked the signal lever of the intercom system connecting the dude ranch with the ranchhouse. Her mother answered so promptly Betty suspected she had anticipated a problem. "Hi, Rabbit," her mother said. "What do you think of the fair Elaine?"

Betty told her the problem.

Her mother laughed. "For goodness' sakes," she said, "handle the problem as you think best. But let me give you a tip. Miss Elaine Robbins and her family were given full and honest information concerning the quarters we offer. Sounds to me as if she's trying to get more than she's entitled to by waxing haughtily unpleasant."

Betty whistled under her breath. A moment later she went back to the tall, beautifully dressed Elaine Robbins and said with more confidence: "It's these quarters or none, Elaine. Actually, we try to give our guests a taste of real ranch life, so we don't offer fancy quarters and the like. I'll be glad to recommend a more elegant place, however. There are some truly beautiful dude ranches around Phoenix and Wickenburg."

The girl compressed her lipss and went back outdoors. Betty tagged along, amused in a way but sympathizing with her, too, because she definitely knew what it felt like to be grossly disappointed. While the girl stood talking to her chauffeur, Mr. Swiftfoot came out for a breath of fresh air and a pipe smoke. He spotted the troubled Elaine Robbins, smiled and went over and held his hand up, palm outward, and said: "How." Next, he walked to and fro before the girl's fascinated chauffeur and studied Miss Elaine Robbins from all angles. Suddenly Mr. Swiftfoot said: "Heap pretty squaw child. Show um gold."

Ah, the crafty old faker!

In no time at all he had Elaine Robbins by the hand and was walking her back to the bunkhouse. "Change um duds," he said. "Chief Snow Eagle get um crowbait horses."

Elaine was laughing merrily by the time he got her to the bunkhouse. "Really," she told Betty, "how clever! I've always been fascinated by Indians. That's why I came here, you know. Next year I intend to write a theme on the Indians of Arizona. What brand is he?"

"Navajo, Elaine. I'll tell you what: now that you're here you might as well give us a try. Say a week. If you still dislike us after a week, I'll personally find you a place more to your liking."

Billy showed up just then, and Betty moved fast to get things settled. She got a suitcase from the limousine and gestured for Billy to get the rest. Billy got even with her, though, inside the bunkhouse. "So this is where all the beauty will spend the summer, huh?" Billy asked. "Shucks, at the Tomahawk Ranch we put our enemies in prettier places."

If he hoped Elaine would notice him, he was well rewarded. Elaine looked him over and smiled. "Cute," she said. "What do you do around here?"

"Run the boys ragged," Billy said.

"But you ought to wash more often," Elaine scolded him. "I must say that you men of the West are a grubby lot."

Billy opened his mouth but snapped it shut in a hurry. After the door had banged shut behind him, Elaine giggled. "I do love to needle boys," Elaine confessed. "They're such self-satisfied dolts, have you ever noticed? They're always sure they know so much, when they really know so little."

Betty laughed, thinking she would enjoy Miss Elaine Robbins very much throughout the summer.

Chapter 10

Within a week, the bunkhouses were filled and the summer season was fully under way. During that first week, Betty saw to it that the guests were introduced to Western life in easy stages, limiting horseback rides to distances that would not tax soft city bodies unduly, limiting swims in the big pool to half-hour sessions so that bad cases of sunburn would not occur. Most of the girls were quite willing to do little but lounge around and make the acquaintance of the fellows. But several were veritable dynamos of energy who had to be watched carefully lest they just ride off when no one was looking and become lost out on the range. To keep these girls happy while the others were adapting themselves to ranch life, Betty led them off one day for a tour of the Lightning W. She timed the tour perfectly, to her intense satisfaction, so that they reached the big breaking corral about two miles out just as a couple of the cowboys and Dan Rawson, the Lightning W peeler, were getting ready for an afternoon's work. Betty got the girl comfortably seated on the top rail of the corral and told them exactly who Dan Rawson was and why he was worth his weight in gold to her father and the ranch cowboys.

"Actually," she explained, "most of the fellows around here are just riders. They're very good, of course, as you must be to work on the range. But if you were to put most of these men on a young, half-broken horse, the probability is they'd be chewing dust in no time at all. That's where Dan Rawson comes in. He specializes as a bronc fighter,

or a peeler. And it's tricky, I'll tell you that.
He has to break or train a horse without
breaking his spirit, or killing him off, as we
sometimes say. Dan is famous in these parts.
He wins just about every rodeo he enters.
And you should see what he does with the
polo ponies we raise and train. Some fellow
back East once said that if Dan wanted to
join a polo team, he'd be rated a ten-goal
man in a year."

Actually, Dan treated them to quite a
show, not because he ever put on a show
but because he happened to draw a truly
spirited mustang. The mustang used just
about every trick in the book to throw Dan.
The mustang climbed for altitude and sun-
fished and jolted and screamed and tried to
bite. The mustang flipped itself over and
tried to smash Dan underneath him. The
mustang raced to the corral fence and tried
to mash Dan's leg against unyielding wood.
But Dan was equal to everything the mustang tried. A veteran of fully a thousand

battles with broncs, Dan stuck to the saddle as if glued. Then, when the horse showed signs of tiring, Dan gave a yip to one of the cowboys at the gate and the cowboy swung the gate wide. The mustang shot for the open range as if swarms of hornets were giving chase. Presently all you could see to mark the existence of horse and rider was a plume of dust shimmering under the hot sun.

The girls were so thrilled they insisted upon staying put until Dan had returned on a thoroughly tired horse that permitted him to pat its head or scratch one of its ears whenever Dan wished to. Later, Betty introduced the girls to Dan, and Dan was kind. He answered every question he was asked, silly or otherwise. Then he turned suddenly and picked up Sue Wiley and plunked her onto the saddle of the next horse the cowboys brought out. Sue gave a shriek you could have heard ten miles off. But did the horse care? It did not. It just stood stock-still, as if it had always known what it was like to have a screeching dude girl on its back. Dan finally turned the horse loose, and it ambled about the corral so tamely that Sue decided it was as safe as any old Dobbin. Sue, and all the others, too, were most impressed when Dan told them that particular horse had been one of the wildest broncs he had ever seen just four months before.

The stirring tale was told and retold within an hour after the return to the dude ranch. Betty, lying on her bed for a much needed rest, was suddenly startled by a thump on her door and then by an invasion of her privacy. Fully fifteen girls in various states of undress piled into her room to demand to know how come she was playing favorites. She was threatened with a ducking in the pool that very afternoon if she did not arrange for all of them to see the bronc fighter in action. And telling these girls that it had just happened got Betty exactly nowhere. She had to dress and go over to the main ranch and powwow with Mr. McWilliams.

He pursed his lips and screwed his weatherbeaten face into a frown. "Pretty big order, that," he said. "I don't see how I can order Dan to risk his neck just to amuse the kids."

Betty nodded, knowing as well as Mr. McWilliams that bronc fighters could be killed or maimed quick as a flash. She did not press the matter, having made the request as she had promised. But it did seem to her that, as official hostess and recreation director of the dude ranch, she was under an obligation to provide the kids with whatever entertainment they wanted. So during the swimming session, while Billy and Manuel kept their eyes on the frolicking, splashing guests, she went over to the ranchhouse to discuss an idea with her mother.

She found her mother thumping away on the piano in the living room. Her mother was playing her favorite piece by Chopin, and she was in such good form that Betty sat down to listen. When her mother finished, Betty applauded. Her mother looked at her and pretended to be quite astonished. "Hmmm," said her mother, "I must be losing my mind. For just a second there I thought my darling daughter was in the room."

"Will you not *do* that?" Betty asked. "Glory, Mom, I'm not a child. If I haven't dropped in often recently, it's because I've been busy."

"Mrs. Foley informs me you've been doing good work, too. All right. Sarcasm withdrawn. We'll assume you love us and love your work. What's the problem?"

"Nothing major," she answered disconsolately. "I thought it would be interesting for the kids to see how broncs are broken, but Mr. McWilliams seemed to think he can't ask Dan Rawson to risk his life just to amuse people."

"How right he is!"

"But I developed another idea, Mom. Couldn't we work out an arrangement for the kids who want to spend a day a week tagging along with the cowboys and other workers? There's a lot to see if you keep your eyes open. And when they went back home, those kids would have a pretty good idea of what real ranch work is."

The idea of course appealed to a woman who had once been a schoolteacher. "I like the idea," she said promptly. "People ought to have every opportunity to see how others earn their living and how the work of each person compliments the work of another person. In fact, I like the idea very much. Suppose I discuss it with your father?"

"And with Mr. McWilliams? That's vital, Mom. There's always risk involved when you're out on the range or even in the fields when the machines are working. It would have to be worked out by Mr. McWilliams pretty carefully."

Her mother's eyes told her she appreciated the subtle point. "All right," she agreed.
"I'll remember Mr. McWilliams' position
and discuss it with him, too."

The doorbell rang as Betty was reaching
for her Stetson. It was one of the boys from
the dude ranch, a short and rather pudgy
fellow with pale city cheeks who looked at
her rather owlishly through the thick lenses
of his tortoise-shell glasses. "Hi," she said,
putting on her professional smile. "You lost
or something? This is forbidden territory."

But her mother called for Vernon Hilton
to come in and show her how a piano really
ought to be played. The boy ambled on
down the hall and into the living room with
the ease of a person who had been in the
house before. Surprised, Betty went back to
the living room. She found her mother bus-
tling about excitedly, arranging the drap-
eries just so to make certain Vernon Hilton
would have the light he wanted at the piano.
"Chopin," her mother begged. "Vernon, I

never hear enough Chopin as Chopin ought to be played. Want something to drink or chew? You name it, and we'll get it."

Not in years, Betty thought, had her mother looked so excited or animated. She looked puzzled at the city fellow, wondering why his rating was so high around there.

He surprised her. "What about you, Miss Stone?" he asked. "Any favorites you want to hear?"

"Sure. What about *Down In The Valley?* I just love the way Ed McCurdy sings that. I must have six or seven of his records."

"Rabbit," her mother scolded, "be your age. We happen to be discussing music, not silly, sentimental folk songs."

Vernon Hilton sat down and struck a chord deep in the bass. Much to Betty's glee, he proceeded to play her request, and he played it far better than she had ever heard it played before, at that. But he did not play it exactly as it had been written. While the melody came clearly to her ears, other things did, too, notes that tinkled or rippled in a way that reminded her of the sounds of water rushing down one of the hills toward the storage ponds. She was utterly enchanted by the tricks his fingers were working with the high, high notes of the piano. Then, powerfully, he struck a series of majestic chords and swung from her folk song to the Chopin piece her mother had been playing when she had first entered the house.

But this was not Chopin music as her mother played it. The notes swirled about her ears in rich floods of sound, now quickening her pulse with their dark quality, now quickening her breath with their sentiment. When Vernon Hilton had finished the song, if song it was, Betty had the oddest feeling she had just gone through one of the most memorable experiences of her life. "Glory," she said from her heart, "you're really an artist, aren't you?"

Chapter 11

Because she recognized in Vernon Hilton a kindred spirit and a fellow artist, Betty took a greater interest in him than was perhaps sensible. A few evenings later she caught Billy with nothing more to do than work on a fancy saddle he had decided to make. She sat down on a bench near the tool and tack shed to watch Billy and to chat. "You must be more useful around your ranch than I am around ours," she commented a bit wistfully. "Mr. Swiftfoot once tried to teach me to make a saddle. No go. I think you have to love saddles to make a decent one."

Billy shrugged. "A person can't do everything, it seems to me. I can't paint pictures, for instance. I'm making this for Mary Foley. She's never had a real Texas saddle. I guess they have a tough time, the Foleys."

Billy worked for a time shaping the saddle tree or frame. It was tricky business, for the tree had to be shaped just so to conform to the needs of both the rider and the horse.

Billy said a trifle apologetically, "I guess I blew my stack with you because I felt so sorry for Mary Foley. It's an odd thing, but lots of times when people have no money other people just can't be bothered about them. Clara says I was wrong to rowel you. Clara says you did your best and that you were the only one on the Board who tried to give Mary and Ben the benefit of the doubt. I guess I should have remembered that."

"It's all right," Betty said. She gazed off at the evening sky. In the west, the sky was almost blood red, and the red seemed to be dripping down the sky to stain the distant desert. But here and there purple could be seen moving in slowly but inexorably, like a mist or a sea. Suddenly some of the kids gathered around a campfire near the boys' bunkhouse began to sing one of the old Western songs. They were led by Elaine Robbins, who looked mighty lovely in her dude Western outfit as she strummed her guitar with all the poise of a regular entertainer. The singing was pretty to hear, and Betty closed her eyes and sat quietly and enjoyed it.

"Ever hear Vern Hilton play the piano?" Billy asked. "I was over at the house the other day and heard that piano played as I never heard it played before. How a guy can get so many notes out of a piano in so short a time I'll never figure out. Your father saw me and came over, and we stood listening for a while. Then he told me that Vern Hilton is a musical prodigy, that he gives concerts in big cities all over the country.

You could have floored me with your little finger. I got the idea he wasn't good for much of anything, that guy."

"What gave you that idea?"

"Well, he's a loner," Billy said soberly. "He can be all alone in a funny kind of way even in a crowd. He doesn't hear what you say, he doesn't see what you see, he doesn't really participate even when he is participating, if you know what I mean. Most of the fellows don't bother with him. Some of the girls tried to interest him, but they didn't get very far. Elaine Robbins really bawled him out because of that the other day. She asked him why he was here if he was too high and mighty to associate with the crowd."

"Really? What did he answer?"

"That was what bothered Elaine the most. After she'd bawled him out awhile, he looked at her as if noticing her for the first time and said yes, it was a pretty nice day if you liked hot weather."

Betty chuckled, having a pretty good notion that Miss Elaine Robbins had been pretty darned vexed.

Billy said a bit nervously: "Without meaning to start another brawl, Betty, he sort of reminds me of you this summer. You're different. You used to be a pretty outgoing sort of girl, lots of fun to be with, the life of the party, so to speak. But you're getting to be something of a loner, too. The kids were talking about it at the pool this afternoon. Some of the girls said they thought you're rather nice when you can be reached. But others said you can't be reached, that you're just as withdrawn as yonder hills."

Betty was interested, not offended. "Really? I hadn't noticed any great change in myself."

"May I be frank, meaning well and all that?"

"Why not? If the Greenleys can't be frank with the Stones, then friendship means very little."

"Well, you're like Vern Hilton in that you participate yet you don't. Here's what I mean. On that ten-mile ride we all took yesterday, you were practically a wet blanket. A lot of the kids were thrilled. They'd never seen hills and the forests before, and they really enjoyed the ride and the scenery. But there you sat, as cold as ice, spouting information about the country as if you were utterly bored."

"I was," Betty said.

"How would you feel, though, if your folks had spent a lot of money to send you here and then some employee took all the fun out of things for you?"

It was a point, Betty had to concede. Her cheeks tingled. She met Billy's gaze briefly, ashamedly, then sighed. "I'll do better," she promised. "It's a sin to be unfair. But getting back to Vern Hilton: what are you doing to help him have a better time?"

"Nothing. What can I do? I'm riding herd on about forty fellows, and that's enough for anyone."

"If I give you Mr. Swiftfoot, could you give him special attention—Vern Hilton, I mean?"

Billy put his tools down, for now it was too dark for proper work. "I wouldn't get very far with him," Billy said bluntly. "I don't understand fellows like him, and I certainly can't talk to him about things that interest him."

Betty pondered this while stars began to appear over the range. It presently occurred to her that it was really her responsibility, anyway. Billy had enough work to do riding herd on the boys and helping the men with various chores. Actually, the division of the work was quite unfair. She could always turn the girls over to one of the cowboys when they wanted to ride farther than she wanted to ride. Being the daughter of the owners of the Lightning W did give her special privileges, after all.

She nodded and told Billy she would handle the problem; then she went over to the campfire and nudged her way into the circle of boys and girls and asked with a great show of enthusiasm if anyone wanted to hear Mr. Swiftfoot tell some creepy Indian stories. The kids whooped with delight, and Elaine loped off to the chuckhouse, where Mr. Swiftfoot had a small room. Mr. Swiftfoot came with great alacrity, but once he was the center of attraction he pretended he knew no stories. He did not get away with this, for these boys and girls were no dolts.

"I'll scalp you!" Elaine Robbins threatened, and at once about six girls and ten fellows stood up and said they would help her. Mr. Swiftfoot then sat down and crossed his legs and got his pipe going. Using his pidgin English act, he said: "Me tell um of owl who wanted to be coyote. Me tell um of evil spirit who wanted owl for dinner, and what happened."

Betty waited until the tale had been well begun. She left the campfire unobtrusively and went across the way to the bunkhouse where Vern Hilton was quartered. At once, one of the dude ranch cowboys came ambling over and said in teasing tones: "Forbidden territory for girls, Miss Betty. Don't blame Clem; blame your Ma."

"Know where Vern Hilton is, Clem?"

"Over at the corral. There's a real strange boy, Miss Betty. None of the kids seem to like him much, but the horses sure love him."

Vern Hilton at once went up a notch in Betty's estimation. She trotted up to the corral in the hills and had no difficulty whatsoever finding the prodigy pianist. He was sitting on the top rail of the corral, generously handing out carrots to the nickering, pushing, grunting ponies. Laughing, Betty joined him on the rail. "Good thing Big Tom isn't here," she told him. "When carrots are up for grabs, Big Tom doesn't tolerate competitors."

"I'd shoot him," Vern Hilton said.

Betty was horrified. "You'd do *what?*"

"I dislike grabbers, Miss Stone. There are too many grabbers in the world."

"Well, there's too much shooting in the world, too. The very idea!"

A sliver of moon came up over the eastern hills. At once the night became beautifully alive with shimmering patterns of silver and shadow. Far off, a coyote began to sing the eternal song to the moon. Betty heard an owl, as well.

"I like nights," she confided. "All this range comes alive at night. Lizards crawl and snakes slither and coyotes run and owls fly. The antelope move around, too, but dawn's the best time for them."

"The sounds are interesting," he said as if making a great concession. "If you put the sounds together just so, you could compose a beautiful song of the West. I'd have that creek over there making the dominant sounds, I think."

Betty asked casually: "Have you ever ridden in the moonlight? It's quite an experience. You feel beautifully alone when you're riding through a moonlit world. I often sneak out for such rides."

He was disturbingly perceptive. He turned a bit to look at her, and he laughed. "Am I a project of yours all of a sudden, Miss Stone? Have you decided to make me enjoy your West? You can't do it. I'm here only because of my nerves. I hate being here. I want to be back East, where people know something about music."

"What's wrong with your nerves, Vern? Oh, and call me Betty. We're not much on formality out here."

"Too many concerts, the doctor said; too much tension. Doctors annoy me."

Betty almost laughed, the remark was so childish. She controlled her amusement, however. "Then you ride with me right now," she said firmly. "If there's one thing the vast, peaceful range can do, it's soothe your nerves."

She hopped down into the corral. Although Vern said he definitely would not go riding with her, she got two horses cut out and headed for the corral gate. When she wanted to get Vern moving, too, she asked quite snippily: "Afraid I'll prove my point, Vern? Does it make you feel important to have a case of nerves at your age?"

Much to her satisfaction, the trick worked.

Chapter 12

The moonlight ride Betty took with Vern
Hilton proved unexpectedly pleasant for
them both. The miles drifted behind them
almost unnoticed, for always they were in-
tent upon the beauty that lay ahead. While
they rode, Vern talked of himself, and in the
process he gave Betty fascinating glimpses
of a world in which music was the primary
art. He had made his debut, he told her, at
the age of nine. Few but his family and
family friends had attended the concert,
even though his mother had given free tick-
ets to just about every person she knew.
"Poor Mom," Vern said, laughing affectionately. "She was torn between pride and disappointment. But the concert went well, and

it so happened that a friend of a New York music critic heard me and liked what he heard. About a month later I received an invitation to play a few classical pieces at a party at the home of this critic. I was lucky a second time. One of his guests was an old lady who practically wept whenever she heard a piece written by Debussy. After I'd played a Debussy she came over to the piano and demanded more and more and more. The critic told me later that he thought I would have a brilliant career as a concert pianist. Naturally, that didn't make me hate him. But I didn't have much money, so I didn't take him too seriously."

"What has money to do with talent?" Betty asked. "You can either play or not play, paint or not paint."

"That's Arizona talking," Vern said with a little laugh. "Having talent isn't enough. Many people who have talent in the arts don't get very far because they need education and training they can't afford. I needed

education and training, all right. I knew it,
too. Whenever people told me I was pretty
good, I'd think of a pianist like Paderewski
or Rubenstein and realize those people didn't
know much about the piano. Anyway, that
critic was partly right. The old lady came to
our house about a week later and told my
mother she wanted to sponsor my musical
education. She turned out to be the Miss
Deborah Peterson whose company makes all
kinds of cosmetics for sale all over the world."

"Glory," Betty said, "talk about luck."

They went up a long slope to a mesa. Now
it seemed as if a billion miles of sky were
stretched all about them. The blazing stars
seemed so near it was difficult to believe you
would not bump your head on one if you
were careless. Sweetly, coolly, a night
breeze struck down from the hills to tanta-
lize Betty with the scents of what her father
had always called, "the never-never faraway
places." Happy to have a good horse under
her and an interesting riding companion

with her, Betty pointed toward some pin-points of light in the distance. "Over yonder is the Lazy L Ranch, Vern. We'll ride that far because I want to show you a mural I helped paint. But I have another motive for taking you there. Our piano is just an old upright Mom has thumped on for years. Mr. Lucas, who owns the Lazy L, has a genuine concert grand piano. He's quite interested in the arts."

"Maybe I'd better not go there, then," Vern said thoughtfully. "I'm not supposed to do any work this summer. According to the doctor, I'm to forget music for a while and open all the pores of my system to life."

"In other words, playing the piano was work rather than fun? I know what you mean. After I'd finished that Indian in the living room, I was plain no good at anything. The cure for that, Mom said, was a dose of desert reality. So Mr. Swiftfoot and I loaded a couple of pack mules and went wandering across the desert for two weeks."

"In all that desert heat?"

"Never noticed it, to be truthful. Why should I? This is my country, you ninny. Does a polar bear ever complain about being cold?"

Vern made a decision. "I think I'd like to see that mural. May I be honest with you? I didn't think much of your Indian because he seemed too stiff and self-conscious to be a real Indian about to brain someone with his tomahawk. But I did like the range and desert pictures your mother showed me. In fact, I bought one."

Betty almost ejaculated: "Huh?" She recalled in time, however, that this childish reaction to surprising news was no longer approved by her parents. "How nice," she finally said. "I hope Mom charged you the limit. Mr. Lockwood tells me that people appreciate only expensive things."

"A hundred dollars."

This time, Betty did say "Huh?" Thrilled, she looked at this boy who had obviously won fortune as well as fame. "That's a lot of money," she said. "Which one did you buy?"

"*Wind in the Sage.*"

Betty had difficulty remembering the picture. She had painted so many pictures of the sage at various seasons of the year.

"The reason I bought it," Vern said, "is that I thought I could hear the wind in the sage. You're pretty good, I think. What I mean is: the wind is invisible, yet in that picture the wind seems to be there before your eyes."

After this news, Betty was quite willing to take him back to the dude ranch. However, they rode on to the Lazy L and found Mr. Lockwood and Jimmy Hayes sitting with Mr. Lucas on the front porch of the new ranchhouse. Mr. Lucas welcomed them with surprising geniality for him, and at once took Vern indoors to show him the desert mural in the rumpus room. While they were gone, Jimmy Hayes gave Betty some interesting news.

"I'm here on business," he told her. "You know what Mr. Lucas is planning to do? He's going to build a little museum in Tincup across the road from the courthouse. Mr. Lockwood is going to run it for him."

"I didn't agree to that, Jimmy," Mr. Lockwood said quickly. "After all, I have a thriving business of my own. But I will confess that I like the idea of a museum dedicated to encouraging artists of the West. There's too little opportunity for artists of today to show their work. How can we expect people to become interested in art if they see little of it? But there are many problems to thresh out before I agree to run the museum."

Jimmy laughed. "I can guarantee that Mr. Bourke will back the idea. He was saying just the other day that Tincup has to become a real city with a museum and an auditorium and all that."

Mr. Lucas and Vern came back. Vern gave Betty a queer look and said so politely she knew he did not mean a word of it:

"That's a beautiful picture, one of the finest I've ever seen."

Betty gestured to Mr. Lockwood, and Mr. Lockwood rose comically and made a little bow. After Betty had told them that Vern Hilton was a famous pianist in the East, Mr. Lucas invited everyone to come inside while Vern took a "whack" at the concert grand piano. Vern tried to beg off, but Jimmy, after Betty had winked at him, grabbed Vern by the arm and laughingly hauled him into the house.

Something wonderful happened.

Once Vern had begun to play on the beautiful concert grand he seemed unable to stop. He played Beethoven and Wagner and Debussy and Chopin and Bach. He played with thunder and he played with such delicacy it made you ache to hear the fragile notes. Once or twice Mr. Lucas called his Mexican man servant to bring soft drinks for the kids and more coffee for the adults. Along about eleven o'clock he also called for sandwiches. And on Vern played, such happiness on his face it was clear to Betty he lived really only for his music. In a strange way, that realization bothered her. There was so much more to living, she thought, than doing the one thing you did really well.

She gave the matter much thought long after she had gotten into bed in her private room in the senior girls' bunkhouse, and she made a decision just before she drifted off to sleep. In the morning, she hunted around for Sarah Tomlinson and took her off alone for a serious talk. "Sarah," she said without preamble, "you like Vern Hilton, don't you?"

Sarah blushed.

Betty chuckled. "Now don't be silly," she chided. "It's natural for a girl to like one fellow more than another. Glory, ask Mom. I'm not saying that at fifteen you should be ready to give your life to him, after all! But what would be wrong with making a little effort to pull him out of that private world he seems to dwell in?"

"I didn't know," Sarah said, "that you ever came out of *your* private world long enough to notice such things about others."

Betty ignored the crack, recognizing that she deserved it. She held her right hand up solemnly. "Me vow big change," she said, mimicking Mr. Swiftfoot. "Me gottum eye-opener last night."

Sarah's blue eyes snapped. "That was a dirty trick," she charged. "A lot of us have been dreaming about a moonlight ride, but you stuck us with spooky stories while you rode off with Vern Hilton."

"I've decided," Betty said, "that things ought to be livelier here. I mean, there ought to be more than just rides and swims and campfires and such. This Saturday we're having a square dance. And from now on we'll have more kids around; town kids you should meet, because they're nice and they're fun. Care to make a big effort to draw Vern out if his shell?"

Sarah gave it thought. She was tempted,

Betty could see, but she was also pretty suspicious.

"How come you don't care to bother?" Sarah asked. "After all, I don't work here; you do."

"Because I can't concentrate on one kid, Sarah, and you know it. But never mind. I'll ask Alice or Kitty or even Elaine."

That did it!

From this success Betty went directly to her parents. She caught them silent at the breakfast table, and that disturbed her. "Hey," she yelled, "what you guys need around here is a daughter. Why the long faces? See the morning! What a beautiful early-August morning! Everybody cheer!"

Her father, Lord love him, at once put down his newspaper and yelled back: "How can we talk when you're making enough noise for a hundred?"

Betty kissed him, kissed her mother, went over to investigate the contents of the refrigerator. She found half a berry pie that looked appealing and carried it over to the table. "Powwow," she announced. "We have some kids at the school who play country music rather well. They could use some dinero. Also, we have some kids at the dude ranch who could use some party entertainment, thank you. What about a square dance every Saturday night? We could use the barn. We could invite kids from far and near. Pop, you can call the dances, and Mom, you and I can serve the refreshments. Agreed?"

"Nope," Ellen Stone said. "Sounds like work. Also sounds like an excuse to get Jimmy Hayes here. Pfui on the big romances of the tender young."

"Well, may Mrs. Foley and I handle it, then?"

That did it! Mrs. Ellen Stone said warmly: "Not even Mr. Swiftfoot's ghosts could prevent *me* from giving those square dances! Do you begrudge me some fun? For shame, Rabbit."

Chapter 13

The announcement was made at campfire that night, and the girls squealed and the fellows pretended not to be interested at all. But the next morning when Betty went with Mrs. Foley to look the barn over, about twenty of the fellow went along. The fellows decided that they might as well be gallant, since all the squaws seemed to be anxious to wear fancy Western clothes and dance. So the fellows took charge of preparing the barn for the festivities.

The girls had a grand time looting the shops for suitable Western decorations, and then all the boys were barred from the barn while the girls worked like beavers for two days transforming the interior into what they thought a Western dance hall had looked like in the olden days. The girls were smarter than the fellows, though. They didn't use their own money to pay for these decorations; they just charged everything to the dude ranch.

Did the ranch queen mind? Not at all! At a conference Thursday afternoon, Mrs. Stone declared instead: "Jerry, I'll want a hundred dollars. That Western dance hall may please the moppets, but it displeases me. We need tables and chairs. We need old bottles and candles. I think I can get what we need from Mr. Jorgenson's rummage shop, but it will have to be a cash deal."

"You want to ruin us?" he asked.

But Betty was more than prepared for that argument. "Pop," she said, "multiply sixty kids by fifty dollars a week. Our gross income is three thousand a week, isn't it? All right. Even when you deduct the salaries of the nine people who work for the dude ranch, you have a lot of money left."

His eyes narrowed. "Yes, but what about the money we have invested in that property? There's a lot of money tied up there just so we can operate a dude ranch ten weeks or so each year. By the time you deduct taxes and cost of the buildings and building maintenance, and food and other supplies, not to forget horses, you find we're not making a fortune."

"But enough," Ellen Stone said, "to warrant the expenditure of a few dollars for entertainment. Better write a check for two hundred. Three thousand a week! Why, I'm feeling positively giddy!"

Betty went to town on this trip. Knowing that the going might be a little rough, she insisted that her mother allow her to approach the Jorgensons alone. While she felt just a bit nervous after they had reached the blacksmith's place of business, she did not allow that nervousness to prevent her from going inside to the forge room.

Near the forge, Ben looked up and saw her first. His father then looked up, crinkled his forehead and put down the hand sledge he had been using to shape some hot metal on the anvil. Mr. Jorgenson rumbled, "Well, girl, I'll say you have nerve. Maybe not good sense, but nerve."

Intuitively, Betty knew that he was far less angry with her than Ben's mother was. But she also knew that smoking the peace pipe with him would accomplish very little, because it was Mrs. Jorgenson who ran the Jorgenson family and its business affairs.

Betty asked for Mrs. Jorgenson. Her request took both by surprise. Each looked at the other as if he thought she had lost her sanity. However, Ben finally pointed toward the little office at the far end of the old wooden building. Betty walked quickly to it and found Mrs. Jorgenson sitting behind a neat rolltop desk, doing book work.

Mrs. Jorgenson said quietly: "Leave,

please. We don't want your kind around."

Figuring she had nothing to lose but her neck, Betty sat down calmly on the only other chair in the office. "What have I done to offend you?" she asked. "It seems to me, ma'am, I have a right to be told that."

"If there's a type of person I can't abide," Mrs. Jorgenson announced, "it's the type that leaves her friends in the lurch."

"I was the only member of the Board," Betty pointed out, "who spoke in favor of a complete investigation. I was outvoted. As for turning down the assignment to investigate the matter: I was up to my ears in school work and art work. I'm not saying I couldn't have squeezed enough time from my schedule to conduct an investigation of sorts, ma'am. But I do say that if I had done that, I'd not have done justice to my school work or my art work or the investigation."

"What was so precious about your art work?"

Although it was not technically any of

Mrs. Jorgenson's business, Betty thought a complete explanation of the whole business ought to settle the matter once and for all. She therefore told Mrs. Jorgensen about Mr. Swiftfoot's arrest for horse stealing and the bargain she had had to make with Mr. Lucas to get Mr. Swiftfoot out of jail. Mrs. Jorgenson finally stopped working. "So that's how come he got out of jail, eh?" she asked. "I wondered. Mr. Lucas never seemed the merciful type to me. He drives hard bargains with my husband, I can tell you that. I don't know that I like him very well."

"He takes knowing," Betty informed her. "If you approach him in the right way, he's really pretty nice. It must cost him a heap of money to support our fine arts classes at the school, yet he never complains. And now he's going to build a museum here in Tincup so that Western artists will have a nice place in which to display their work."

"He can afford it, the prices he pays my husband for shodding those thoroughbreds of his. Still, I have to say it'll be nice to have a museum. I like to see real pictures. Well, what do you want? Why didn't you tell me all this before? Oh, no matter. What do you want now?"

Betty told her. Mrs. Jorgenson was interested for two reasons: first because the sale would be a big one for her to make, and also because Ben picked the liveliest banjo you could find in Tincup.

"You paying for the music?" Mrs. Jorgenson asked. "You can't expect the boys to work all evening for free."

"We thought we would pay each musician a dollar an hour, ma'am."

Mrs. Jorgenson jumped up excitedly, a short and scrawny woman dressed in an old gray skirt and sweater. She called for her men folks to come hear the news. When it became evident to father and son that the Jorgensons and the Stones were friends again, both fellows loosened up considerably and promised to do their best to get chairs and tables and the sassiest music around for the kids to dance to. Betty was able to report complete success to her mother a few minutes later.

On Friday, the desired tables and chairs were brought by truck. Some looked pretty disgraceful, but Betty accepted them and then spent much of the remainder of the morning helping a couple of the men clean them and arrange them in the barn. In the afternoon, she went to her room in the ranchhouse and got her private telephone directory from her desk drawer and telephoned invitations all over Tincup and the nearby vicinity. This chore kept her busy for several hours, because each kid she called had a lot of questions to ask about her summer and then had a lot of things to tell her about his summer. Some of the news was particularly interesting. From one girl Betty learned that none other than Miss Betty Stone herself, was being considered for the presidency of the Students' Disciplinary

Board for the coming school year. Betty at once protested that she was definitely unqualified, but this girl said it was up to the student body, not the candidate, to decide such matters. One of the boys had even more interesting news. He told her that Jimmy Hayes had been given a promotion and was now officially a cub reporter on the *Tincup Ledger*. Betty was thrilled deeply and lost no time calling the newspaper office to congratulate Jimmy. But instead of Jimmy she got Mr. Bourke himself. Mr. Bourke laughed when he recognized her voice. "Just the girl I want to talk to," he said. "What's all this I've been hearing about that piano-playing guest of yours, Vernon Hilton?"

"Mr. Bourke," Betty said from the heart, "he's a pianist who can thrill you to the core."

"What about letting me run a story about him? I don't get a chance to write about real celebrities more than two or three times a year."

Betty chuckled and then invited *him* to attend the square dance. To her astonishment, he actually came.

Indeed, everyone who had been invited came, and others who had not been invited. They came early, while the sun was still going strong and while dust devils were dancing around the range. Moreover, everyone came in fancy Western attire and high spirits, and in no time at all the dude ranch kids and the local kids were chattering away and laughing as if they had known one another all their lives. Once Betty had seen to the introductions, she had little to do but enjoy the party herself. She hunted Jimmy down and cold-bloodedly detached him from a couple of girls who had come dressed like Western gunfighters. She curtsied most prettily to Jimmy, and he rose to the occasion by bowing most expertly over her hand. "But I'm not sure," he said, "that I like you in a dress like that. You look like a spinster lady from another age. What's the big idea?"

"Because I work here, goop, and it isn't polite to outshine the guests. And may I say I dislike you in the getup of a gambler? You should be a cowboy, Jimmy, a knight of the old West."

"I will *not* be a cowboy and I will *not* ride a horse."

But now the music began inside the barn, and Betty's father jumped up and yelled for the Grand March indoors to begin. Boys and girls and quite a few adults laughed and got into line. And now, magnificently, the musicians inside began to play, "Oh, Susanna!" in so lively a way that you suddenly wanted to dance with your fellow or your girl all the night through.

Elaine Robbins grinned as Betty and Jimmy got into line behind her. "I'll say this for you," Elaine told her. "When you come out of those long, long thoughts of yours you make a gal glad she came to Arizona. Such fun! Wheee!"

Then into the barn they marched, and the dancing began, not to end until midnight with everyone standing in a big circle and singing *Auld Lang Syne*.

Chapter 14

Betty awoke the next morning with a delicious sense of well-being, and she dressed for the day with a happiness she had not felt in months. She went directly to the chuckhouse to eat with all the other employees before the guests got up and complained they were starving to death. While she ate, she discussed recreation activities with Billy Greenley. She had, she announced, decided to have a camp-out. Some of the girls had been pestering her for one, she told him, and it seemed high time they obliged their guests. Billy looked pained. "It can't be boys and girls together," he insisted. "That would be rough work. Some of these kids have pretty advanced ideas on what the moonlight is made for."

"Mush-slush?" Betty laughed.

"It's no laughing matter," Billy said seriously. "I have news for you. That girl you palmed off on Vern Hilton actually told me she was going to marry him or bust."

Betty was incredulous. "Sarah Tomlinson?" I can hardly believe it! Why, she can't be a day older than I!"

"If that. Boy, did I tell her off. I said that at her age she ought to be thinking about her studies and things like that. But can you blame her? Her mother married this June for the fourth time . . . that's why Sarah is here for the summer. I guess to Sarah marriage must seem some kind of game."

Betty promptly altered her plans for the camp-out. "Girls one night, boys another. How's that?"

"Fine," Billy said. "He grinned. "Girls first, since I'm such a gentleman these days."

"Boys first," Betty told him, "to make certain there aren't snakes and such in the camp grounds."

But there was an incident anyway. When the boys rode in from their camp-out several mornings later, Vern Hilton was conspicuously absent. Billy and the wrangler Manuel and the cowboy Clem were quite upset. Clem reported that he had spent half the night looking for Vern and that they had finally decided Vern had ridden back to sleep in the bunkhouse. Billy went to look, and there Vern was, quite unconcerned about the worry he had caused them. To Betty he said, "I don't love your West so much I want to sleep out in it under a tent." He also announced that he had made arrangements to do some serious practising at Mr. Lucas' place each afternoon and that from now on she could just forget his existence.

Betty was puzzled. This was hardly the friendly fellow with whom she had ridden one night. He seemed cold as ice. "Forbidden!" she said as crisply as possible. When Vern tried to protest, she went outdoors and informed the fellows that under no circumstances was Vern to be given a horse or any other form of transportation without her express permission.

But the night she led the girls off for their first camp-out Vern Hilton got away anyhow. Billy came riding to the camp grounds around midnight to give her the news. All the girls squealed the instant they recognized his voice. Scandal! they squealed. Shoot the invader down! Betty thought fast in the emergency. She whooped for Elaine and put her in charge of the camp. She ordered Billy to stay at the camp, scandal or no scandal, to make certain a wandering coyote or antelope did not frighten the girls silly. She got aboard Big Tom and rode disgustedly off across the range to the Lazy L. She kept Big Tom moving, not looking around at the beauty of the Arizona night.

When she reached the Lazy L she gave the front door one thump with her fist and then went inside. There was Vern, all right, playing for the crusty Mr. Lucas. When Mr. Lucas realized she had entered without permission, he stood up angrily. "You go too far," he said. "You get out of here before I put you out."

"Sorry," Betty apologized, "but this is serious, sir. Vern, do you ride back or do you leave the dude ranch? It's up to you. We can't assume responsibility for you, that's all."

"Crazy, chattering females!" Vern yelled. He stood up, his eyes wild, his face beet red. "How can I play the piano if I don't practise? Are you jealous, Betty Stone, because I'm famous and you aren't?"

Betty swallowed and looked at Mr. Lucas. She said quickly, "It's his nerves, sir. His doctor sent him here because of his nerves."

For once, Mr. Lucas talked with what Mr. Swiftfoot called a honey tongue. "Boy," he said, "easy does it. This girl rode here alone because she was worried about you. The least we can do is be polite."

With the help of Mr. Lucas, Betty finally persuaded Vern to return to the Lightning W with her. But she took him to her folks' home rather than to the dude ranch. After Vern had been taken upstairs by her father, Betty discussed the problem with her mother.

"He's loco," she said, beginning to feel angry now that he was off her hands. "Do you know what he does, Mom? He actually retreats to his music whenever things don't go as he wants them. I guess Sarah Tomlinson has been pestering him too much. Sarah told Billy she was going to marry Vern or bust. The dope must have taken her seriously."

"Send Sarah to me in the morning. Of all things!"

"We'll either have to send him back East, Mom, or I'll have to give him special attention. It's all right, it seems, when he's with me. We discuss art and such, and I tell him about the land and the Indians, and he gets pretty interested."

"Well, you're the boss. What do you suggest we do?"

It gave Betty a peculiar sensation when she realized her mother was actually referring the matter to her for decision. She started to nibble her lower lip, but stopped when she saw the storm light gathering in her mother's eyes. "Golly," she said at last, I'd have to think about it. If he wasn't someone pretty special, I'd clout him with a club and tell him to grow up. We all have to do things we don't want to, but do we carry on like he does?"

"In our individual ways, I'm afraid some of us do," her mother said dryly.

Betty understood her mother's point. She flushed. But she could not say, as her mother obviously wanted her to, that she had decided the decision about Chicago and the art lessons had been neither unfair nor arbitrary.

"The fact remains," she said stiffly, "that I am here and I don't have a case of nerves, Mom. Personally, though, I think I could straighten Vern out if I could give him special attention."

Her mother asked practically: "When would you have the time? It appears to me that you're doing more and more each day. And while we're on that subject, what about your personal social life and your art? Your father and I have noticed you see none of your friends, take no sketching trips to the hills."

"Time enough for that when school begins. I'm not miserably unhappy, incidentally. It's fun to chat with the different girls and fellows, to learn about their lives, their values. Anyway, someone has to do something about Vern, or send him home."

"What about hiring an assistant, Betty? I'm sure Clara or someone else would like to earn a few dollars. Say you were relieved three or four hours each afternoon? What you did with your free time would be your concern. If you wanted to spend it with Vern, fine. If you wanted to take him on sketching trips, that would be perfect. I dislike your neglect of your art. Mr. Lockwood told me just the other day that he thinks you may be able to become a good artist if you work hard at it."

Betty had an inspiration. "What about Mary Foley?" she asked. "Clara doesn't need the money, but Mary does. Mary knows the country, and she has a fine personality. The girls would like her."

Her mother gave the girl's tanned, serious face a long inspection. Ellen Stone asked with gentle diffidence, "Trying to buy your way back into her favor, dear?"

Betty smiled faintly. "I guess so, in a way," she admitted slowly. "But I like to think I'm also trying to make amends. I'll tell you this much. Next year, regardless of

my schedule or what anyone thinks, I'm
meeting every issue head on and fighting
every battle to a conclusion."

"That's the idea, Rabbit. In life, you do
what you must do. When you learn to accept that, you're on your way to becoming a
fine person. Very well. Mary is on the payroll, and you have four hours to yourself
each afternoon, beginning today. I'll relieve
you until Mary comes to work."

A couple of days later Betty took Vern in
tow. It was strange. Although he was a bit
older and much more famous than she would
probably ever be, she felt not at all back-
ward about blistering him with her tongue
when he told her he did not want to go
watch her sketch. "You're a baby!" she
charged. "The trouble with you is that you've
been fussed over and pampered much too
long! Well, here's one little mother who will
clobber you with a rock if you try any tan-
trums with her. Get on that horse or I'll
scalp you bald!"

The dozen or so kids within earshot looked at her as if they disbelieved their ears. But infinitely more important to Betty was the fact that Vern appeared to believe she would scalp him bald. He climbed onto his mount so quickly it was comical. But Betty did not laugh. She nodded at Mr. Swiftfoot, and the old Indian led them off to the desert. Although the sun was fiery, they did not stop to rest until they had entered the dry, mostly bare hills. Vern kept sputtering and complaining, and Betty kept ignoring his behavior. She identified cacti for him and she pointed out a lizard to him and then she gave him a real treat—showing him holes in a big saguaro cactus that were used as nests by pygmy owls. Vern, of course, was too intelligent not to be impressed by the strange beauty of the desert. After they had gotten in among the hills he stopped his sputtering and complaining. Indeed, after they had dismounted near a red and blue-green draw Betty wanted to sketch, Vern ambled about quite energetically, inspecting rabbit brush and mesquite and the always present sage as if seeing them all for the first time. It was not long before old Mr. Swiftfoot was telling him many things about the desert, and the first thing Betty knew the fellows were wandering off, presumably to investigate the wide, wide world.

Contented, Betty got her sketch pad and charcoal pencils from her saddle bag and sat down to sketch the draw.

Chapter 15

For Betty, the next two weeks were perfect in every respect. The weather was sizzling hot, exactly as she loved it. The kids at the dude ranch knew enough by now not to take silly chances on the range or even with the cattle or horses. It was possible for her to put especially reliable kids in charge of others and then to allow independent trips under the watchful eyes of one of the cowboys or Mr. Swiftfoot. Then, in the afternoons, it was possible for her to turn the girls over to Mary Foley with a guiltless conscience. With all the high jinks taken out of them by their morning activities, the girls were quite content to lounge around the pool or the bunkhouses throughout much of the afternoon. Mary, a lively redhead, complained one afternoon, "They're really so tame, Betty, I feel ashamed to take a dollar an hour for sitting with them."

Betty was happy to hear the girls were so well behaved, for the knowledge made it possible for her to ride out each afternoon with Vern with not a single worry in her mind.

And those afternoon trips! After the first three or four she found Vern always waiting for her, the horses saddled, food and water in the saddle bags, and a big anticipatory smile on his face. Wherever she wanted to go was just fine with Vern. One day they went to an Indian village. They were met by barking dogs and running kids. Betty got several of the kids up onto Big Tom with her, and Vern, not to be outdone, did the same. Then they all went to the cluster of shacks that comprised the village. While

Vern ambled around looking at everything, Betty found the old Navajo lady she wanted and sat down to sketch her weaving a blanket. The old lady was kind, as always. Not even her eyes, usually so eloquent, once betrayed amusement when Betty stumbled over a word she could not quite pronounce correctly. The old lady said her way with the language was good. The old lady then proceeded to ask questions about Vern, who seemed to amuse her because he looked so solemn with his big, round eyes behind his thick-lensed eyeglasses. When Betty informed her that Vern was a famous pianist, the old lady went into her shack and brought out an old crank victrola and put on some records for Vern's benefit. Betty did not have the heart to tell her Vern played classical music, not pop stuff. And Vern, the nice fellow, complimented the lady not only on her skill as a weaver but also on her fine taste in music.

Another time, Betty took Vern to the

Mexican section of Tincup. They went by
jeep for a change, and Betty wore a simple
white cotton dress, her best nylons and well
polished shoes. Vern said her costume made
him feel shabby and then asked what the
occasion was. Betty, chuckling, explained,
'The older Mexicans think it's indecent for
girls to wear slacks or shorts in public, silly.
Well, I darned well wear what I wish on the
ranch, but when I visit someone else's place
I naturally pay them the courtesy of dress-
ing as they think girls ought to dress. We're
going to see Manuel's sister. Do you think
you can make beautiful music? Well, just
wait until you hear Maria play the guitar
and sing."

In the Mexican quarter, Betty told Clem
to take the jeep and do what he liked for the
next couple of hours. She then took Vern's
hand and led him along under striped awn-
ings and through hot, spicy smells to the
little restaurant run by Manuel's parents.
Maria came with a fine burst of Spanish and

much laughter to welcome the "little pigeon" to a great feast of enchiladas and coca cola. The fact that Betty could jabber away with Maria in Spanish left Vern very much impressed. "Where do you learn these languages?" he wanted to know. "Navajo, Spanish . . . and what else?"

"That's it. And, actually, I don't deserve any credit for knowing a smattering of them. Don't forget that Mr. Swiftfoot had a hand in raising me, and don't forget we have lots of Mexicans working for us. You know, Indians and Mexicans are the kindest and warmest-hearted people to children that you'll ever meet. When I used to run in the fields, there was always a Mexican fellow to make sure I didn't stumble into an irrigation ditch and drown. Or take the desert. I got too big for my britches once when I was nine. I rode out to the desert alone, believe it or not. Was I in any mortal danger? Pfui! Practically every time I looked around, there was an Indian keeping an eye on me!

I was indignant. I shouted for them to go away, that I wasn't a baby any more. So do you know what they did? They politely kept their eyes on me but made sure I couldn't see *them*."

While Vern was laughing, Maria came out of the kitchen with piping hot enchiladas for them to try. Betty begged her to play and sing. Maria kissed her. "For my most ardent fan," she said, "I shoot the works!" She got her guitar. She stamped her foot, struck a chord that sent thrills through Betty, and then she all but exploded into sound and action, singing a lively song about the adventures of a runaway burro and practically acting out his every step and his every encounter with things and creatures strange to him. Pretty soon men and women drifted into the small place and took all the chairs and yelled, "Ole!" each time a particular note or step pleased them.

Vern seemed to be having the time of his young life. He kept time with his right hand,

listened intently for a while, then went over
to the old piano in the corner and insisted
Maria do the burro thing again. Much to
Betty's astonishment, he was able to accom-
pany Maria without making any mistakes to
speak of. What was more, he managed to
enliven the already lively song with runs on
the piano that flashed brilliantly up to the
highest notes and then came down, down,
to end in "clip-clops" that sounded for all
the world like the striking of the burro's
hoofs on hard ground.

In the end, Vern repaid Maria for her
concert with a concert of his own. And it
was interesting to Betty to notice that he
played far more beautifully for this audience than he had played for Mr. Lucas. It
seemed to her there was warmth in his playing this time, as if he were playing the
music because he wanted to rather than because he had to. She enjoyed the concert so
much she yelled, "Ole!" with the audience
when Vern had struck the final chord of the

final crashing crescendo.

And so it went throughout those two perfect weeks. Betty felt absolutely at one with life, and everything in life pleased her. The teasing of the girls in the senior bunkhouse each night could be endured and even laughed at, because she had a deep conviction that what she was doing with and for Vern Hilton was right. This time, at least, she was not turning her back on someone's emotional need. Knowing that, and knowing that she was meeting the responsibility to him she had assumed, made her impervious to teasing even when there were needles in some of the comments made by Sarah Tomlinson. Every afternoon of the two weeks was spent with Vern regardless of what anyone said, and if he got much from the activity and the daily association, so did she. Each afternoon she completed at least one sketch, complete with color notes, and on more than one occasion she rose around four in the morning to do some painting in her studio before the dude ranch kids rose to claim her time and attention.

Oddly enough, it was this reawakening of her interest in art that brought the perfect two weeks to a close. One Sunday afternoon, Mr. Lucas and Mr. Lockwood and a Mrs. Myra Foster came unannounced to the Lightning W. Betty was called to the house after the visitors had been there about an hour. She answered the summons as she was, and the woman who turned out to be Mrs. Myra Foster gave her mother an odd look and said: "If she was mine, Mrs. Stone, I'd tub her. How on earth can one scrap of a girl get so dirty?"

But this was said with a laugh. Betty was asked to show Mrs. Foster her paintings, and Betty dutifully led her to the barn studio. Mrs. Foster climbed the ladder quite well for a city woman. When she saw the racks of canvases, she even said: "Worth every second of the risk and effort." She spent almost two hours looking over the paintings, dismissing some with scorn and others with such comments as: "You almost got that" and "Good analysis but careless execution." It occurred to Betty, naturally, that her work was being appraised by a bona fide art critic, and it therefore interested her to notice that now and then Mrs. Foster put a painting off to one side without making any comment about it one way or the other.

Presently Mrs. Foster said she had seen enough. She gazed about the studio. A couple of the Navajo blankets and rugs hanging on the board walls brought envy to her eyes. "Excellent pieces, those," she said. "Not the sort of thing an average tourist ever has an opportunity to buy. The genuine article; the honest work of people who have made a high art of weaving. Do you want to know something, young lady? I find the same honesty in your work. You have much to learn, no doubt of that. But you see things as they are, and you're honest enough to paint them as they are. The result is that you put a most interesting and even exciting wild West into every painting. You love your home country, don't you?"

Betty nodded, feeling much encouraged by the fact that Mrs. Foster had found honesty in her work. To her, that was the vital thing. She knew that if she just worked long enough and hard enough, she would some day master such difficult things as composition and anatomy. But honesty was something almost impossible to learn. That was something that was either ingrained in your makeup or not. In her opinion, the talent to see truly was just as important as the talent to draw or paint anything at all. And if God had given you that talent, she thought, you were very lucky and had every justification for thinking that in time you might paint a few things worthy of the attention of intelligent people.

Mrs. Foster said, "I think you ought to go to Chicago this autumn, Betty Stone. I'll tell your parents so. Also, I'll tell Mr. Gifford that I will accept you as a pupil. You'll have to work, I'll tell you that. I don't teach the lazy, the indifferent, the people who go into art because they think it's exciting and glamorous. But if a person has the basic ability and the desire to learn . . . well, fine. Now, then, suppose we take that junk of yours out of Mr. Lockwood's window and replace them with these paintings I've selected. These are excellent. I'm buying *Grand Mesa* for my own collection."

Betty said, deeply thrilled, that Mrs. Foster could have the painting for free. Mrs. Foster laughed. "Lesson number one," she said: "a good artist always grabs every dollar that's offered her."

She paid for the picture before she left.

Chapter 16

It was Jimmy Hayes, the "reporter who knew everything," who told Betty exactly what had happened and why it had happened. She met Jimmy quite by chance in Tincup after she had helped Mr. Lockwood place the paintings chosen by Mrs. Foster in one of the big display windows. Jimmy called to her from the doorway of one of the shops and came hustling over to her, his right hand out-stretched. "Congratulations," he said. "Betty, I couldn't be happier if it were happening to me."

And this was true, Betty saw. Here indeed was one person who rejoiced sincerely in the good fortune of another. He was a fine person, Jimmy Hayes, she thought. She was darned glad that she knew him.

"How did you find out?" she teased. "My, what a successful snoop you're becoming!"

He put on a comically stern expression and shouted in imitation of his editor, Mr. Bourke: "It's the duty of a reporter to learn the news even *before* it happens, young man!"

Betty giggled. "Dolt!" I don't know how you manage to write such wonderful stories. How do you, Mr. Cub Reporter?"

"Well, I'll tell you how it is," Jimmy said. "First, I find something to write about. Then I investigate, or snoop, as you call it. Then I go home and sit in front of my typewriter and work. About five hours later I manage to have two or three pretty good paragraphs written. The next day I show those paragraphs to Mr. Bourke. He says, and I quote, 'Very poor, Hayes; very amateurish.' Then he rewrites those paragraphs. And that's how I write those wonderful stories."

"Something tells me," Betty said, "that you're a bit better than you admit. Don't forget that I've known Mr. Bourke for years. He wouldn't bother with you if he didn't have a high opinion of your ability."

"For those kind words," Jimmy said, "I'll give you the story behind the story of Mrs. Foster's visit to your home."

It was an interesting story Jimmy told over cokes in Pop Reardon's drugstore. One day, it developed, some friends of Mr. Lucas had looked at the desert mural in his rumpus room. Suddenly one of the friends, a naturalist, had cried: "Why, how perfect!" He had shown Mr. Lucas a pair of eyes peeping out from a hole in one of the saguaro cactus plants. Mr. Lucas had been both dumbfounded and pleased. The naturalist had gone on to say that the artist had given him the first genuine painting of the desert he had ever seen. That had done it! Mr. Lockwood had been called to the ranchhouse. Mr. Lockwood had informed the company that he could take no credit for the subtle touches that made the picture seem almost to live on the wall. The upshot of it all had been a decision by Mr. Lucas to "get that talented little lady off the range before a horse throws her and kills her." So Mr. Lucas had gotten into touch with Betty's parents. From them he had gotten Mr. Gifford's address in Chicago. He had told Mr. Gifford bluntly that someone ought to be sent West to examine the girl's work critically, and he had gone on to say he would pay the expenses of the critic who was sent.

"So there you are," Jimmy said. "I got most of the story from Mr. Lockwood. And right there, for my money, is a very great man. You know how it is with a lot of adults. They're inclined to think that because you're sixteen or so you're pretty stupid, all in all. But not Mr. Lockwood! He didn't take credit for the work you did. And he even told Mr. Lucas that he wished he had your basic ability. He said you're just about the best natural artist he's ever met."

"Pfui," Betty dismissed this praise. "Any time you want to see the poorest work in Arizona, you let me show you some of my human beings."

Jimmy smiled. "Yes, they're pretty poor. I guess you're as poor at painting them as I am at trying to write the first paragraph of a newspaper story. You know what, Betty? You and I are more or less in the same boat. We have an awful lot to learn, haven't we?"

"But it's fun to learn, isn't it?"

"You bet. I wish, though, that you were staying here this year. When things don't go well, it's nice to have someone around to talk things over with; someone who knows what it's all about."

Betty had her own opinion as to where she would spend the next year, but she kept it to herself. Nor did she discuss the matter with anyone else in the days that followed.

She continued with her work at the ranch quite as if Mrs. Foster had never paid her a visit, working with the girls in the mornings, continuing her special work with Vern Hilton in the afternoons. It was her thought that, with the season drawing to a close, she ought to forget other matters until September. She did strive to forget them, but was only partially successful.

One afternoon Elaine Robbins invaded her room while she was changing into range clothes. Lovely Elaine said, "What a modest mouse you are, Betty. Heap proud Indian chief tells me he's going to Chicago with you this autumn to help you study painting. How exciting! And Vern Hilton tells me you'll be a lot more famous than he one day. May I have your autograph?"

"Hush, chatterer. Darn it, I don't like to think of autumn. This has been a grand summer, all in all."

"So wonderful," Elaine said, "that I've already reserved my bunk for next year.

How amusing! The day I arrived I thought this was such a dull dump."

"That's the West," Betty told her proudly. "Some of it may not look like much when you first see it, but it grows on you. Care to go riding with us this afternoon? Vern is quite civilized now."

"These fellows," Elaine said, laughing. "They think they're so much stronger and braver and wiser than we females. But notice who it is that has to cure them of whatever it is that ails them? You've done a fine job on him, incidentally. He was the life of the party last Saturday night. But may I ask one little question? Why have you bothered with him? You work hard, all of you here. Why take on more work, especially when it isn't your responsibility to turn a character into a nice human being?"

Betty stuffed the tails of her shirt into her levi trousers. She slipped her feet into her boots and reached for her Stetson. "Very easily answered," she informed Elaine. "Last

March I learned a lesson I'll never forget.
The lesson is that it's everyone's responsibility to do what he can to help anyone who
needs help. If it weren't for a fine teacher,
Mrs. McCracken, two nice kids would have
been disgraced when they should have been
honored. Ugh! Never again! Now I do what
I can the moment I can."

Elaine decided that she would accom-
pany Vern and Betty, but as it turned out
it was a good four hours before they could
find Vern. When they went to the corral,
Manuel, the wrangler, gave Betty the star-
tling news that Vern had come early for his
horse and had gone galloping away, tears in
his eyes and rolling down his cheeks. Manuel had tried to stop Vern, but what could
he do there on his own two feet instead of
upon a horse?

Some quick questioning of some of the
boys who shared bunkhouse 3 with Vern
brought out the information that Vern had
received a disturbing letter that morning at

mail call. "He yelled that he wasn't going home," Betty was told. "He said he was going to live his own life for a change."

Grimacing, Betty rejoined Elaine Robbins. "A long hard ride," she said. "Apparently Vern got news that disturbed him and took off to lick his wounds out in the great beyond. It's over near Lonesome Butte, ten to one, that the wound licking is being done."

Elaine threw her head back and squealed with laughter. "Ah, these big, rough and tough fellows we girls always have to straighten out!"

They rode. Hot though it was, they rode steadily and with a lot of conversation that gave Betty a fine insight into Elaine Robbins' character. Elaine's family was quite wealthy, she discovered, but she also discovered that neither Elaine nor her parents took that very seriously. Elaine, it seemed, was determined to be a nurse one day; hence the delight she took in the knowledge that it was to girls fellows turned when life was just too much for them.

They found Vern where Betty had expected to find him. He was sitting on a flat rock gazing off at miles of sage that twinkled every time the wind blew across the land below. The soft sounds of their horses attracted Vern's attention. Without turning around, he said: "Ah, don't scold me, little artist. I'll go East. I'll play with that symphony orchestra at that music festival. But you won't make me like it. This is what I like, so don't argue with me, please."

The girls dismounted. Elaine took a seat beside Vern and asked him what he saw out there in all that nothingness. He gave her a surprised look. "How come it takes two girls to catch one fellow?" he asked.

"Sometimes it does," Elaine said. "Anyway, I wanted to come. I happened to enjoy the new Vern Hilton last Saturday night. I wanted to make sure, I guess, that he wouldn't run back into that private world of his. When do you have to leave for that concert?"

"Day after tomorrow."

"Big surprise?"

"Big surprise. Someone else was scheduled to play, but became ill. My agent thought it was a good chance for me, so I fly back and play for free. And I haven't practised seriously in weeks!"

Betty sat down on the other side of Vern. "If you don't know how to play now," she pointed out, "you never will. Oh, I know what you're talking about. If I don't paint for a few weeks I become rusty. But a day or so takes the rustiness out of my system. Why don't you scoot over to the Lazy L before supper? I'm sure Mr. Lucas will turn the concert grand over to you. Spend the night. Spend all day tomorrow there. Then take the plane. Do some more practising when you're home. You'll be all right."

Vern nodded, taking off his eyeglasses. "I'll be all right," he agreed. "I know that. A month or so ago, if you'd told me I could climb onto a horse and find my way here, I'd have called you crazy. But I did it, and somehow I have the feeling I can do anything I have to do."

"Sure you can," Betty told him. "According to my Mom, you can do whatever you want to do if you just want to do it badly enough. Well, shall we ride back to the dude ranch?"

Vern said: "Shush, you range boss. Don't you know what I'm doing here? I'm composing. I'm finishing a tone poem called *Wind In The Sage*. But how do you finish an impressionistic piece such as that?"

Elaine laughed. "Very simple, Mr. Composer. What happens at close of day? A wind springs up; a wind that cools the land and brings a thousand sweetnesses to your nostrils. The creatures who live on the range wake up and begin to move about. So you play that. And don't you dare forget the sage rippling in the wind. See it now! End of day coming? Sure. End of summer coming? Sure. So there's the end of your tone poem, as well, with lots of rippling notes, Vern; with lots of bouncing notes for the antelope, too; and lots of slithering notes for the snakes and lizards. And then it all fades away as the days do here, and there's the moon, and there are the stars, and there's the memory in everyone who sees this place or hears your tone poem of a perfect day, a perfect summer."

Something perfect happened right there before Betty's eyes. Vern looked at Elaine and said in a voice of wonder: "Then you understand, too? Darn it, why didn't I get to know you better this summer?"

"Well, maybe next summer," Elaine said. "And of course you could come see me in Delaware this autumn and winter if you're in the vicinity."

Vern said he would see her, all right. And he would, Betty knew, just as she knew that she herself would see much of Jimmy Hayes

in all the long years of her future. Nothing
else was said. They got onto their horses and
left the rippling sage and the butte for the
last time.

Chapter 17

For Betty, her first summer of hard work and heavy responsibility actually ended that afternoon in the wild country with Vern Hilton and Elaine Robbins. Although she continued to work dutifully and efficiently until the final day of the season, her job no longer seemed vital to her, a challenge she had to meet foursquare to demonstrate to herself as well as to others that she was not just a child incapable of sustaining a serious interest in anything. Riding back to the dude ranch with Vern and Elaine, she had the oddest notion that she had just turned a corner in her life. The notion became conviction in the days that followed, and as the conviction developed thoughts of the future filled her mind. She was anxious to come to grips with her future. A girl practically sixteen had not time to waste, especially if she wanted to devote her life to art. The sooner she could pop into a tub and wash summer from her bones, the sooner she could buckle down to serious work. One thing she definitely wanted to do was another portrait of Mr. Swiftfoot raising his tomahawk high preparatory to giving a death blow to a mortal enemy. It was preposterous for a person who hoped to be an artist to be baffled by such a thing as plain anatomy!

But she stuck it out determinedly until the last campfire songfest of the year. Each day she led the girls out for long rides across the ranch so that they could see the beginning of the late-summer roundup. She had sole charge of the girls now, because every cowboy on the ranch was needed for the important business of gathering the cattle together preparatory to shipping them west to the Los Angeles market. Some of the girls presented problems. Excellent riders now, they were eager to participate in the round-up. One girl said with shining eyes: "Imagine me being able to tell my folks I actually helped to round up honest-to-good-ness steers!"

Betty pointed out crisply that the work was dangerous. "Those steers have roamed the range since spring, you idiots. They're wild! If they had the chance, they'd trample you!"

But one morning about a dozen girls decided to help the cowboys anyway. They spotted about fifty head of cattle ambling along the edge of an arroyo, and off the girls galloped, whooping excitedly. Betty's blood ran cold, but not for long. Suddenly, to her intense delight, the riders fanned out and skillfully worked the cattle away from the arroyo. Then, with many yells and much

hat waving, the girls got the cattle moving
at a good clip across the range in the general
direction of the shipping yard. Not once did
any rider get within a hundred feet of a
steer. Forming a giant U, with the lead
riders almost abreast of the lead steers, the
girls simply kept the herd tightly together
and maneuvered it through the gates of the
shipping yard as neatly as if they had been
doing such work all their lives.

Mr. McWilliams, who had witnessed the
operation from start to finish, was clearly
impressed. "Girls," he yelled, "I'm signing
you on here and now. I want four hundred
more head before Friday."

Naturally, the girls did some mighty cute
swaggering before the boys at the campfire
that night. Thinking they had earned the
right to swagger, Betty let them brag. And
although Billy suggested that maybe she
was taking too many chances, Betty allowed
the same dozen girls to work the range the
following day. She was darned proud of

them, and to show it, she went to the house late that afternoon to bum some spurs free of charge from her mother.

Her mother was amused, but promised to buy some spurs in town for presentation to the glorious range riders at the last campfire. Moreover, her mother made the presentation herself, spouting a pretty little speech while the tongues of flame leaped and danced in the clear crisp air. "Girls," she said, "here in the West we have a saying that it isn't easy to earn your spurs. And that's a true saying, because it takes more than the ability to ride to do a proper job of rounding up range cattle. You must have good judgment, perfect self-discipline, the courage to retreat as well as to charge. So, of course, I'm very much pleased that so many of you have become qualified to wear a real cowboy's spurs; not dude spurs. And when I remember that most of you knew little about such things when you came here, I must say that I'm greatly impressed by your accomplishments."

She then called each girl by name and formally presented her with a set of flashing spurs and welcomed her into the Lightning W Order of Sourdoughs. There was much cheering when the last presentation had been made, and there were also many vows from the less expert riders to do better, much better, next season.

Then Betty's mother made a final announcement that thrilled her to the core. "One final item," her mother said, "and then we'll douse the last campfire of the season. The item concerns Vern Hilton. As you know, he left the ranch early to play the piano at a music festival in the East. Vern did himself proud. According to the newspaper story I read, he received a standing ovation that lasted twenty minutes. And then Vern did us proud. For an encore, he played a tone poem of his own composition, a piece he calls *Wind In The Sage*. Vern was pleased to dedicate the piece to my daughter, and apparently it thrilled everyone. One critic wrote that he thought the piece so magnificent it stirred in him a desire to travel West to see the country that had inspired the music. Heap big praise, that, don't you think?"

Betty had to leave, because silly sentimental tears were forming in her eyes as they always did at the last campfire of the season. She ambled off through the dark, hearing Mr. Swiftfoot behind her, following her as usual to make certain no harm came to his beloved Golden Hair in the night. She was a bit annoyed with him.

"I'm not a child any more," she told him. "I'm practically a woman now, and women don't need guarding."

He laughed softly, gently, understanding her pride, her independence. To tease her, he went into his pidgin English act. "Boy heap brave buck now, Golden Hair. Good. He came here baby; he go home man. You do um good job."

Off behind them, the girls and boys began to sing old songs. Beautifully the voices came to them, and Betty told the old man to shush and sat down on one of the bunkhouse steps to listen to the singing.

All in all, she thought, feeling both happy and sad, it had been a wonderful summer. If Vern had found himself, so had she. Never again would she rant or rage or sulk when she was stuck with a job she did not want to do. Nor would she ever again doubt that she was capable of doing whatever work she was compelled for one reason or another to take on. If some of the summer had been rugged emotionally, much of it had also been rewarding. Twelve of the girls had won their spurs! All of the kids had a good time! Billy Greenley liked her and respected her again! Mary Foley was now her fast friend! Mr. Swiftfoot had behaved all summer long! And from Vern Hilton she had received as much as she had given him . . . a tone poem!

"I'm lucky," she told the old Indian. "I'm one of the luckiest girls in the world, did you know?"

But the old Indian had returned to the campfire, no doubt to tell the kids one more ghost story before they headed for their bunks. Amused, Betty decided that it was time that she left, too. She got Big Tom from the dude ranch corral and rode off to the main ranchhouse. At around ten o'clock she went up to her room looked around the place and thought: My, how sissy! But she loved being there again amidst all the pretty colors and frilly things. Laughing, she got out of her rough range clothes and scooted into the pink-tiled bathroom and treated herself to a carnation bubble bath in the big tub. She remained in the tub until the water turned cold, then rinsed herself under the shower and put on her fancy lime-green nightgown and negligee. She was doing her hair before the vanity-table mirror when her father knocked. After he had come in and sat down on the straight-backed chair near the wall, she went on brushing her hair. "This year," she told him, "I'm going to be a glamour girl. It's strange, but that thought kept running through my mind all summer long. Think you'll enjoy all the fellows who always come flocking to see a glamour girl?"

"It'll be a switch, at any rate. I don't know that I'll be able to stand the shock of clean fingernails and perfectly brushed hair and all that."

Betty decided that this was as good a time as any to get the important thing settled. She swung around to face him, her tanned face very serious. "I won't go to Chicago," she said, "if I have any choice in the matter. Ever since Mom made the announcement about Vern Hilton, I've been thinking that this is my world, the place I ought to remain in. What can I be taught in Chicago, Dad? Many technical things, of course, sure. But will Mrs. Foster be able to teach me what the desert looks like in autumn? Will she be able to tell me that at this or that time of day the distant hills turn gray and purple and seem to recede farther and farther into the distance?"

He pursed his lips and shrugged. "Parents are rough on kids, I'm afraid. They don't intend to be, but circumstances seem to force their hand. Take now. What emotion inside you is compelling you to say these words? Is it fear? Are you afraid you can't hold your own in Chicago? I think Vern was unhappy here for a while because he was afraid."

"Nonsense," Betty said sharply.

"Now as for leaving the West," her father said, "how can you? This is where you were born and raised. You have sand in your craw and the smell of sage in your nose and a love for the wide open spaces in your blood. This is a part of you, Rabbit. No matter where you go, what you do, how you live, you'll always have the West with you, because you are the West, don't you see?"

"Next year, Dad? Vern is right, darn him.

I know nothing about doing decent pictures of human beings. I need to study anatomy, and Mr. Lockwood can help me. I need to know other things, too, if I'm not to have a one-track mind all my life. I need to be president of the Students' Disciplinary Board. I need to talk to fellows like Jimmy Hayes and Billy Greenley. I need to learn what makes Eloise Quayle tick, and—"

Betty broke off because her mother came into the room. She met her mother's twinkling eyes and nodded proudly. "That was the loveliest gesture, Mom," she said. "Those girls must have been thrilled when you presented their spurs. I know I was thrilled."

"Glad you were satisfied, boss lady. I'm also glad you've decided to stay here another year. Oh, I heard you. And I think you've made an intelligent decision. First things first. Education is a must, and I'm not referring to education in art alone. Frankly, I think you ought to complete high school and then go East. But let's be clear on this subject once and for all. I think, to be honest, that you earned your spurs this summer, too. So if you want to study under Mrs. Foster in Chicago, I'll put you on the train myself, with my blessings."

The compliment pleased Betty, but she did not allow it to make her heady with pride. "Ma'am," she teased, "I'm right proud you like your daughter. I'll do you a favor and stick around until I've graduated. There, how's that?"

Her mother did a rare thing. Her mother caught her in a hug that made Betty's ribs hurt. "You boss lady, you!" her mother cried. "Really, you did a wonderful job right from the start. And your work with Vern . . . well, that was a work of art, too! A dress, a dress, I insist on buying you the most elegant dress you've ever had! If people are going to dedicate fine music to you, I don't want you slouching around here looking like a saddle tramp."

Betty's eyes shone.

Her mother laughed and released her. "Oh, that reminds me, dear. Put on a dress, will you, and tell Jimmy Hayes this is *not* the time for a boy to call on a girl? He covered the closing campfire ceremony for the newspaper, and now he's downstairs waiting to interview you."

Betty's heart began to thump. She told her folks to go downstairs to make certain that Jimmy did not become bored while waiting and leave.

Then she dressed slowly, carefully, knowing that even if she took an hour Jimmy would wait. How interesting, she thought, that for years and years no one really noticed you, and then all of a sudden you were worth waiting for, and someone came along to wait!

Her face radiant, a song in her throat and in her heart, Betty took one final glance at her reflection in the mirror, then put summer behind her and went downstairs to chat with Jimmy about her plans for the autumn and winter.

Her appearance dazzled poor Jimmy. "Say," he asked, very suspicious, "are you giving me the treatment?"

Her folks laughed and left, but Betty did neither. "A girl has to practise," she told him solemnly. "How am I doing?"

Jimmy, of all things, was speechless for once!